Avril Tremayne is an ~~~~~~~~~~~~~~~~~~~~~~~
modern, urban romanc~~~~~~~~~~~~~~~~~~~~~~~
enough to make any w~~~~~~~~~~~~~~~~~~~~~~~
heroines who neverthe~~~~~~~~~~~~~~~~~~~~~~~
a circuitous route to be~~~~~~~~~~~~~~~~~~~~~
in nursing, teaching, public relations and corporate
affairs—most recently in global aviation, which gave
her a voracious appetite for travel. She currently lives
in Sydney, Australia, but is feverishly plotting to
move her family to Italy for half of every year. When
she's not reading or writing Avril can be found dining
to excess, drinking lots of wine and obsessing over
shoes. Find her at avriltremayne.com, on Facebook
at avril.tremayne, on Twitter, @AvrilTremayne, or on
Instagram, @avril_tremayne.

If you liked *Getting Lucky*, why not try

Close to the Edge by Zara Cox
Beddable Billionaire by Alexx Andria
Forbidden Pleasure by Taryn Leigh Taylor

Discover more at millsandboon.co.uk

GETTING LUCKY

AVRIL TREMAYNE

MILLS & BOON

First Published in Great Britain 2018
by Mills & Boon, an imprint of HarperCollins*Publishers*
1 London Bridge Street, London, SE1 9GF

© 2018 Belinda de Rome

ISBN: 978-0-263-93230-0

MIX
Paper from
responsible sources
FSC® C007454

This book is produced from independently certified FSC™ paper
to ensure responsible forest management.
For more information visit www.harpercollins.co.uk/green.

Printed and bound in Spain
by CPI, Barcelona

For my wonderful, supportive, honourable husband,
without whom there would be no books.

CHAPTER ONE

ROMY RANG THE DOORBELL, and a few seconds later, heard a "Cooooomiiiing," from somewhere inside.

It was hard to believe that this house—or was *mansion* the correct word for Russian Hill?—was Matt's. To say it was a departure from his usual student-like accommodation was a whopping understatement.

An inside door slammed. A closer "Gotta find the keys" was called out, followed by an even closer, much louder "Fuck!"

Okay, it was *definitely* Matt's place.

She ran a neatening hand over her hair while she waited for him. Unbuttoned her overcoat. Brushed at the flared skirt of her new red dress.

Stupid, really. Matt never noticed what her hair looked like or what she was wearing. He saved such observations for women he wanted to have sex with—and Romy had come to terms with not being one of those women ten years ago.

Still, her natural inclination was to look immaculate-but-fashionable for business discussions, and the deal she'd made with Matt on the phone two weeks ago was definitely in that category, despite the chaos of that crazy call. Serious enough to warrant a flight from London to San Francisco to dot every i and cross every t.

Footsteps on floorboards. A fumble at the lock. Another "Fuck" that had her battling a giggle, because it was so typical of Matt to be impatient with a door that didn't open fast enough. A click, a swoosh…and there he was.

Six feet three of lean, hard muscle looking rebelliously casual in just-snug-enough jeans and a just-tight-enough T-shirt; hold the footwear because he never wore shoes unless he had to. Good-looking in a boy-next-door-meets-fallen-angel way. Thick waves of red-blond hair, sharply alert green eyes, incongruously olive skin. Tick, tick, tick, tick and tick—Matthew Carter was a prime genetic specimen.

"Good evening, Mr. Carter," Romy said, tamping down another giggle at the absurdity of assessing Matt's attributes like he was breeding stock. "I'm here to discuss your sperm."

Matt gave her a censorious tsk-tsk at odds with the twinkle in his eyes. "I hope you don't say that to *all* the boys, Ms. Allen!"

"Only the ones with a really big— Matt!"—as he yanked her over the threshold and into a fierce hug.

"A really big what?" he asked, digging his chin into the top of her head. "Go on, I dare you to say it."

"Cup, you pervert," she said, dissolving into laughter even though her bottom lip was suddenly trembling from the emotional toll of being on the cusp of something momentous with him. "A really big *cup*!"

"Cup?" he scoffed. "More like a bucket! We're talking serious size and don't you forget it!" He released her, looking down at her with a grin that promptly faded.

"Uh-oh, do *not* cry! You know you look like a troll when you cry!"

"Trying not to," she said shakily. "It's just…you're just…you're going to hate me for saying it again, but you really are my— Hey!" as he dragged her in for another hug.

"If you call me your fucking hero one more fucking time I'll squeeze you hard enough to crack a fucking rib!"

"Okay, *okay*!" Watery chuckle. "Enough fucking!"

"There's never enough fucking to suit me, you know that." And as she chuckled again, "But I mean it, Romy. It's one hybrid kid. Not like we're spawning a dynasty of Targaryens to rule the Seven Kingdoms."

"Except I feel like I'm carrying the iron throne in my briefcase," she said, wrapping her arms around his waist. "Weighs a ton."

"Briefcase?" He half and half laugh/groaned. "Tonight is going to suck sooo badly."

"A briefcase *which you made me drop*. Serve you right if it gouged a hole in your floorboards. And you're squeezing me hard enough to crack *two* fucking ribs, by the way."

He dug his chin into the crown of her head again. "Keep complaining and I'll bench-press you!"

"You'll give yourself a hernia."

"I've been working out—I can take you."

"You haven't seen my backside lately! It's expanded. Way bigger than anything you're used to."

"I'll look at it if you want me to, but as an expert in all things posterior I usually start by copping a feel," he said.

"Hmm, well, I've eaten enough to feed an army in

the past two days and I'm fit to burst out of my clothes, so maybe just take my word for it. I wouldn't want to shock you."

"You always eat enough for an army, so don't try using that as an excuse for your butt—*or* for not cooking the paella you promised me, if that's where you're heading."

She choked up again, because paella was a pathetically inadequate thank-you for what he was doing. She searched for words to express her gratitude more eloquently, but she knew he wouldn't let her say them—he *never* let his friends thank him, always brushed them off, said it was easy, he was doing it for himself, no big deal, anything to shut them up—so she simply rested her cheek against his chest and...ahhh...breathed. In, then out, in, out.

"It'll be all right, Romy, I promise," he murmured into her hair.

"You always say that," she said huskily.

"Because it's true."

Romy smiled against his chest. Matt's *It'll be all right, I promise* had become a group slogan in their Capitol University days. He'd said those words to her, Rafael, Veronica, Artie when he couldn't run away fast enough, and even the older and more rational Teague, whenever he was trying to convince them to do something off-the-wall. Skydiving, bungee jumping, that outrageous sex-in-a-public-place challenge, the horrendous pub crawl during a near blizzard, flying all the way to Sydney, Australia, for a *weekend* to support Frankie the Aussie barmaid when her bastard ex got married, skateboarding down Lombard Street the time they'd all come to San Francisco to hear Matt speak at that tech conference and he needed to release some energy. An endless stream of dares that had them following Matt like lemmings off a cliff because whenever he said *It'll be all right, I promise*, they believed him. And even though such adventures mostly *didn't* end up all right in the end, they'd lemminged after him the next time anyway, because Matt was invincible.

But this time, *this* dare, the consequences were forever. And while Romy wasn't so much willing to embrace those consequences as desperate to do so now the carrot had been dangled in front of her, she couldn't bear the thought that this might be the one time Matt wound up regretting something.

Already, though, she was ready to believe things would be as all right as Matt promised. That was the effect he had on her, probably because he was always picking up her pieces, whether they were fully broken, slightly chipped or just a little bit scratched.

She closed her eyes, blocking out everything except the smell of the arctic pine soap he always used, the feel of his chest rising and falling with his breaths, the well-washed texture of his T-shirt beneath her cheek, his hand pressing between her shoulder blades, bringing her closer. So close her heart felt bruised against his hardness. No...not bruised, squeezed. Squeezed until it was pounding. Pounding until she was dizzy.

And then she realized Matt's heart was pounding, too, and the world tilted. A rush, a swirl, a blaze of heat, and she was in territory that was both familiar and *un*familiar—like she'd been pitched into a color-saturated virtual reality. A picture darted into her head. The two of them chest to chest and hip to hip against the wall, Matt's mouth on hers, his hand fumbling her skirt up out of the way, his fingers tugging at her underwear, and then… Oh God, *God*, he was big and hard and sliding into her until she was full of him, stretched and throbbing and wildly wanting. *You want my sperm, then take it, Romy, as much as you need, take it all, but take it like this.* Her legs wrapping around him, jerking in time with his thrusts. *Yes, please, Matt, please.*

"Matt, please!" she whispered, tilting her hips into his as though what she saw in her head was hers for the asking, for the *taking*.

Matt went perfectly still, and so did she as reality clubbed her back to her senses.

Long moment of nothing but hectic heartbeats and held breaths. And then he let her go so suddenly she stumbled back and almost fell over her briefcase. He grabbed her arm, righted her, released her abruptly again.

Romy, frantically replaying that fantasy in her head, knew how that breathy *Matt, please* must have sounded—like a woman on heat. Nothing new for Matt, who'd been beating women off with the proverbial stick ever since she'd known him, but definitely new between the two of them. And Matt's holy-fuck-help-me expression was telling her their status quo wasn't about to change.

"Sorry, jet lag," she said—the first excuse she could think of. "It kicked in last night, and I barely slept so I've been feeling light-headed all day. I guess when you squeezed me like that, it made me a little…a little woozy. A little…breathless…?"

Okaaay, best case scenario would be for Matt to grab her in a headlock, rub his knuckles against her scalp and tell her to stop bullshitting him, because she'd been flying between the UK and the USA for ten years without suffering from jet lag, so she should just confess—ha-ha-ha—

that she'd thrust her hips at him like a nymphomaniac because she wanted his body. To which she'd respond— ha-ha-ha—that being part of a harem wasn't her style and he should stop wanking over himself. The same comedy routine they'd been doing since the night they'd met to ward off any vaguely sexual frisson that might oscillate between them.

Worst case scenario would be… Hmm, well, that would be what he was doing now. Closing his eyes, then bolt-opening them as though he'd seen something horrific behind his eyelids. Smiling like he was trying not to throw up. *Agreeing* with her, "Yeah, jet lag's a bitch." And then reaching past her to close the door with the air of a guy who'd dislocate his own arm if necessary to avoid contact with her.

About the only good thing to be said for such a response was that he was obviously intent on ignoring her momentary lapse into oversexed insanity—praise the Lord!

She bent to fiddle with the clasp on her briefcase, buying herself a minute to recover, reassuring herself that all she really had to do to get past this episode of utter mortification was not thrust her hips at him like a nymphomaniac *again*. Should be easy enough: she'd had ten years' practice pretending not to lust after him.

Fixing a smile on her face, she took her briefcase by the handle and straightened—and if she was daunted to find that Matt had taken himself out of touching range, presumably for his own safety, at least she had enough self-control to keep smiling.

"We'll talk in the library," Matt said, looking at her right eyebrow. "Through here." And he opened a door to the left of the entrance hall and fled.

Romy dropped her briefcase again—and her smile with it—covering her face with her hands to trap the groan she just couldn't keep inside. She wasn't sure she'd cope if he started addressing all his remarks to her eyebrows. Deep breaths. More deep breaths. Phew. She slowly lowered her hands—and then drew in a few *more* deep breaths as she finally noticed the grandeur of her surroundings, which were definitely in the mansion-not-a-house category.

The floors were a chocolatey-dark wood, the walls painted low-sheen gold. Two impressive staircases curved their way to an upper floor. Behind and between the staircases were two massively proportioned doors, closing off what she presumed was the living area. To the right was a door matching the one Matt had gone through to get to the library.

She tilted back her head, expecting to find a chandelier hanging from the ceiling, and even when that was exactly what she found, she couldn't quite believe it. All that was missing was a gigantic vase of exotic flowers on a marble table and Matt's entrance hall would rival the lobby of the five-star hotel she was staying in. Her entire flat, with its jammed-together living, dining and kitchen areas, would fit into this one space.

She tried to imagine the library, using this as an example, and decided she couldn't actually get past the fact that Matt *had* a library. He only read ebooks! How did an e-reader require an entire room?

Of course, Matt had only moved in a week ago; the first she'd heard he was even looking for a place was when he'd emailed her three days after her fateful phone call, asking what he'd need to set up his new kitchen. So the library was probably just an empty room waiting to be repurposed. Or maybe it was nothing but a grandly named study housing a desk, a couple of chairs and his computer paraphernalia. Because *libraries* weren't Matt's style. *Libraries* were what the Teague Hamiltons and Veronica Johnsons of the world had in their homes. And not because Teague and Veronica were any more loaded than Matt—by his twenty-seventh birthday last year Matt had made a fortune selling the online payment software he and Artie (his partner in all things geek) had built while still at college. It was more that where Teague and Veronica carried the suggestion of the bred-in-the-bone wealth that went with stately homes, self-made Matt was just Matt. He still drove a beaten-up Toyota, still wore Levi's, T-shirts and Vans when barefoot wasn't an option, still drank Sam Adams.

A curse floated out to her through the doorway on the left, followed by a thud.

Ha! And he still swore like a sailor and had the patience of a gnat.

She reached up a hand to pat at her hair. Took off her overcoat and gave her dress a more thorough brush down. Adjusted the silicon-lined band at the top of one of her thick black thigh-high socks, which had slid down half an inch. Re-pasted her smile. Picked up her briefcase.

Showtime.

CHAPTER TWO

Fuck, fuck, *fuck*.

It had seemed so easy two weeks ago. A favor to a friend. On par with what he'd done for Romy back in their Capitol U days, when they'd all lived on top of each other in Veronica's town house and there'd been no hiding the fact that menstruation was more a feat of endurance for Romy than a normal bodily function.

He, Veronica and Rafael had taken turns refilling her hot water bottle, making her cup after cup of Lapsang Souchong, breaking the megawatt-but-useless painkillers out of their blister packs, restocking her why-are-they-disappearing-so-fast sanitary items. Even Teague had taken a few turns, despite not living with them—during *and* after his brief stint as Romy's boyfriend.

So when Romy had called two weeks ago to update him on where she was at with getting her whack job of a uterus fixed, it was pretty much a case of business as usual.

Or it *would* have been, if Camilla hadn't answered his phone.

Women he was fucking always seemed to need to do that when Romy's name flashed up, so it wasn't the act of answering the phone that bothered him so much as the way she'd said, *Oh*, *it's your Romy*, before swiping to accept the call.

His Romy? Fuck that! Romy was just Romy.

And then Camilla had told Romy that Matt would call her back, and that was a step too far in the proprietary stakes so he'd pulled the phone out of her hand fast enough to give her whiplash of the wrist and taken it into another room.

Camilla had looked mightily displeased, but it was poor form for a guy to ask a girl about her menstrual cycle in front of someone she'd never met, so he'd left Camilla to it and launched straight into it with Romy via a short, sharp opener: *Enough of this bullshit, how do we fix it?*

We can have an ablation, she'd said.

Then have one, was his response.

She *couldn't* if she wanted a kid one day—which she definitely *did*, she'd explained—because there'd be no having one afterward.

So have a baby now, he'd said, what was stopping her?

Little problem of no man in her LIFE! And yes, she'd screamed the last word, because a cramp had ripped her in half at that exact moment.

He'd paced the floor while she'd breathed through the pain, and then said, fuck it, *he'd* give her a baby—why not?

And she'd said, *Why not?* Because it was a big deal requiring more than the *one minute's* reflection he usually afforded life-and-death decisions.

And he'd told her it sure as hell didn't require her usual *one thousand years'* reflection, *and* that it would make the top ten list of easiest things he'd ever fucking contemplated: a quick ejaculation on his side of the

Atlantic, a turkey baster on hers, a courier in between, a baby at the end and Yippie-Kai-Yay motherfucker to the problem.

She'd laughed so hard at the *Yippie-Kai-Yay motherfucker* she'd snorted, but she was crying at the same time, and then she'd said he was the next best thing to Captain America to offer, even if she couldn't accept.

And *he'd* snort-laughed then, insisting that Captain America was a *virgin* as well as not being the masturbatory type, whereas Matt had shot out so many gallons of semen over the years—with and without the assistance of a second party—he could have his own page in *Guinness World Records* so where was the comparison?

And somehow during the ensuing argument over Captain America's sexual expertise—or lack thereof—which they'd been having forever—Matt's sperm offer had been accepted and general terms for proceeding agreed to, and he'd felt pretty damn happy with himself because hey, he was going to be a father, which he'd *never* thought he'd be.

Correction: godfather.

Because *obviously* he couldn't be a *real* father.

By that stage Camilla had left, presumably in a huff since he hadn't heard from her since, and Matt had figured that was just as well since she probably wouldn't appreciate his commitment to impregnating another woman even if he wasn't actually coming within spurting distance of Romy's fallopian tubes.

And now here they were, and he felt pretty sure Camilla had jinxed him with the *his Romy* bullshit because *his Romy* wasn't the Romy he'd opened the door to.

His Romy had obviously been kidnapped by aliens and replaced with a metamorphosed porn star version who looked exactly like *his Romy*—neat and chic, clean and bright—but was on a mission to drive him out of his fucking mind with the need to get his hands on her. Which he *could not do*, because *his Romy*, his *real* Romy, was off-limits.

He wasn't *allowed* to imagine taking *his Romy* against the wall energetically enough to shake the crystals off that god-awful chandelier. He would never have flung *his Romy* halfway across the hall for fear of what he might otherwise do to her! Because he would never have mistaken *his Romy's* breathless *Matt, please* as an invitation to enact that shameful scene in his head when it was really nothing more than a plea to stop his rampaging dick from stabbing her in the stomach—and thank God she hadn't called him on that but had taken pity on him by blaming a mythical case of jet lag for the whole damn disaster.

And okay, taking the blame for him was something *his Romy would* do, which meant she really *was his Romy* and his alien abduction theory therefore was a bust.

The only other explanation for this whole phenomenon was that it was an aberration brought on by his two-week sexual hiatus—and the fact he'd lasted two weeks without sex, ever since Romy's phone call, was the equivalent of *him* being abducted by aliens and replaced with a *choirboy* version of himself!

Matthew Carter a choirboy? Now, *that* was an aberration.

As he'd hurried into the library and manhandled his chair into the best position for hiding the beast in his jeans under the desk—not without a certain amount of cursing and desk-related violence—he'd decided it probably wasn't unusual for sex addicts to crave the first available person they saw during periods of deprivation. Didn't mean he was going to act on it, though. He'd been keeping Romy safe from his perversions for ten whole fucking years and that's how things were going to stay if he had to lock a chastity belt onto her himself!

What the hell was keeping her, anyway? They should be halfway through her first document by now. The tedium of paperwork would put a stop to any weird-ass sexual cravings, so he wanted those damn documents stat! Bring them *all* on, the whole fucking briefcase full!

He checked the time on his cell phone. She couldn't be lost between the entrance hall and the library—only one door in the corridor was open and she'd have to see not only the glow of the lights but feel the heat from the monstrous fucking fireplace that was slowly stewing him in his own juice.

Maybe he should go and find her.

Take her by the hand...lead her upstairs...into his bedroom...strip her...lie her across the bed. Ash-brown hair tangled on his pillow...eyes a glitter of hazel from beneath those heavy, tilted lids that made her look perpetually, deceptively sleepy...mouth slightly open as she panted for him...tongue darting to lick her top lip... breasts round and heavy...beige nipples jutting proudly... thighs opening to reveal her pink, juicy core...waiting for his fingers...his tongue...his cock. A whimper, a moan, as he slid inside her...clenching around him... hips rising to meet his thrusts...

Oh God, he wanted to come...needed to come.

His heart was thudding the way it had in the entrance hall when he'd had his arms around her, his shoulders tightening, thighs clamping, his dick straining for release. And then the hairs on the back of his neck vibrated themselves upright as though a lover's finger were trailing down his spine, and he realized he was no longer on his own in the room.

He focused his eyes on his cell phone, counting out the seconds, willing himself to get it together before turning to confirm Romy's presence behind him... aaand go...

He swiveled his chair, and lust rushed at him like a bullet. He wanted to suck the breath out of her, rip the clothes off her, lick the scent from her skin.

What the fuck was happening to him?

"Sorry to make you wait," she said, her trying-but-not-quite-making-it smile telling him she felt his tension. "I had to call Lennie to report on last night's restaurant."

She'd taken off her overcoat, and when she paused on her way to the desk to drape it over a chair he saw what she meant about bursting out of her clothes—her bodice was skintight, and she looked ripe as a ready-to-eat-immediately peach. He really didn't think he was going to survive tonight.

"It's two in the morning in London," he said, the snap in his voice a symptom of his overwrought edginess.

"So?"

"So don't try telling me you called Lennie." Not that it was anything to *him* if she called Lennie at two in the fucking morning.

"I...I did," she said, and blushed, defensive. "Chef's hours. I couldn't have called him any earlier."

"Yeah, well, Lennie's an asshole, expecting you to report in after every meal," he grumbled, and swiveled his chair back to the desk, because the blush pissed him off and he didn't want to see it. Not that it was anything to him who she blushed over, but she shouldn't be blushing over Lennie of all people. "You're a restaurant consultant not a slave."

She'd reached the desk and took her seat, holding her briefcase on her lap as though it were that chastity belt he'd told himself she needed. "You know I have to jump when he says jump."

"I know you can't trust a guy who fricassees garden snails," Matt said, because *he* didn't trust Lennie. Lennie thought he owned her.

She gave an agitated little huff that told him he was being a dick. "And here I was thinking you might have given up burgers for escargot."

"Why would I do that?"

"The house...this room." She looked around. "Your tastes have changed."

"It's just a library."

"Yes, and it's very *library*-like," she said, looking around again. "Hmm. It reminds me of the library in Teague's family's place in the Hamptons. All those shelves full of...of books."

"Hel-lo! Library!"

"Yes but the chairs, tables, Persian rugs, velvet curtains. That fireplace! Big enough to incinerate an elephant!" She laughed, but it sounded forced. "Remember that time we were all invited to the Hamptons for the Hamiltons' Fourth of July ball? Even Veronica was wowed by the library!"

"You went into raptures over it, too, so what's the problem here?"

She grimaced—*grimaced!* What the fuck!

"I just...wondered if you'd bought the place already furnished, that's all," she said.

"Why? Because I don't have Teague's good taste?"

"Well, you *don't*, actually. Nobody does! But what I meant was that not even *you* could get all this done in a week."

"Oh." He shrugged, suddenly self-conscious that it *hadn't* been furnished, that he'd hired people to do it, that he'd told them to copy Teague's style and to get it ready in a week in time for Romy's visit. The library, the kitchen, two bedrooms—his and a spare in case she decided to stay—and an outdoor table, two chairs and a patio heater so they could eat breakfast on the deck tomorrow, because the deck wasn't as oppressive as the rest of this fucking ginormous house. And now it felt all wrong. "Look, are we going to spend the night talking about decor or can we get on with the business at hand?"

"Okay!" She huffed a breath in and out as she pulled a sheaf of pages out of her briefcase and put the briefcase on the floor beside her chair. And then she frowned at him. "You know all this paperwork is only to help you make an informed decision, right? I'm not here to torment you with red tape."

"I'm not tormented."

"You sound tormented. You look tormented. You—"

"I'm not tormented!"

Pause. "Let me put it a different way."

"Fuck!"

"If you're having second thoughts about giving me your sperm, I'll let you off the hook, no questions asked."

He almost laughed at that! "Romy, I'm having so many thoughts about giving you my sperm I can barely keep up with them—but not one of them involves being let off the hook."

"I just want us to be…you know…normal."

"So we make that a nonnegotiable condition, okay? We stay normal or it's off."

"Yes, but—"

"Jesus, Romy, move things the fuck along or I'll think *you're* having second thoughts!"

She opened her mouth, closed it, opened it, closed it, opened it, and all that drawing attention to her mouth was not helping because it made him want to kiss her! And then, "Fine!" she said. "Fine. If you're sure." She sorted agitatedly through her paperwork. "Here," selecting a page and holding it out to him as she placed the rest on the desk in front of her.

He took the page. "What is it?"

"A waiver my lawyer drew up for your protection."

"Protection from what?"

"From me. Think of it as the prenup you have when you're not getting married."

"You've got to be kidding me!"

"I'm not going to have people say I baby-trapped America's favorite dot-com billionaire."

He stared at her for one long, fraught moment. And then, "Okay," he said, and read the document. "Right." Looking up. "Got it."

"Read it again."

"I don't need to read it again, Romy."

"Yes, Matt, you do. You make decisions too quickly. And this is important. Important enough that you might want to have your lawyer read it. In fact, you *should* get your lawyer to read it."

"I don't need my lawyer to read it, because I'm not signing it."

"Well, of course I'm not expecting you to sign it right this minute."

"I'm not signing it, period."

"What?"

"Will this make it easier to understand?" he asked—and ripped the page in half, dropping the two pieces back onto the desk.

"Why did you do that?"

"Because if you think I'm going to sit here on a fortune while my kid lives on a budget on the other side of the world, you've got rocks in your head. I may know fuck-all about being a father, and we both know I'd be a shitty role model for a kid—"

"You would not!"

"—but one thing I *can* do, and do easily, is money."

"I don't want your money, Matt."

"The money's not for you, so get over it. You're getting just about everything you want out of this deal, Romy, and that's fine. That's great. I'm cool with it. But for the love of God, stop rubbing in the whole I-don't-need-you-Matt thing."

"Rubbing—? Need—? I don't—!" She peered at him as though trying to dive into his brain. "I don't understand. All I'm trying to do is protect you!"

"I don't *want* to be protected. I just…" He stopped, dragged in a slow breath. "I just…want to do this."

"You *are* doing this. You're providing half the chromosomes."

"Yeah, anyone with a dick can do that."

"But I want *your* dick," she said.

They looked at each other in shock—and then they both burst out laughing. And God it felt good. Back to normal. Almost.

"Is that a Freudian slip?" he asked. "Because hey, come on over to my side of the desk."

"Oh, shut up."

"Look," he said, "seriously, what difference is it going to make if I fling you a few dollars? I could support a hundred kids and not notice the outlay."

"It's not supposed to be about buying a baby."

"I'm not selling one."

"It's not *fair* to you. Not when you'll have a real family one day."

"You *are* my real family. You, Rafael, Veronica, Teague, crazy Artie."

"You know what I mean. What happens when you get married?"

"I'm not getting married. No other kids. This is it for me. My one chance. So don't take it away from me over something stupid like money."

"Are you blackmailing me?"

"I'm appealing to your kind heart."

"You are so full of it!"

"Okay, I'll switch to blackmail if you're going to be mean about it. I'm making it a nonnegotiable condition of my participation. No money, no kid." He picked up the pieces of paper. "Now, are we starting negotiations on the same torn page, or not?"

"Blackmail isn't a negotiation."

"Ticktock, time's a-marchin'."

"Yes, but it's my clock that's ticking, not yours. You have all the time in the world to have other kids."

"Don't want others. I'm good with clocks. Might as well synchronize my alarm with yours. Are we on? Decide."

"I don't— I can't— I'm not...not *like* that. I don't make decisions on the fly."

"But I *do*, Romy. And things work out just fine for me. So decide. Now."

Long, long moment. And then, "Okay," she said, the word sounding as though it had been dragged out against its will. "I'll take the money, but I want it tied up in a trust. I mean it, Matt. No sneaky stuff. No saving me from imaginary destitution on the sly. I'm getting my lawyer involved—I'm warning you."

He dropped the paper pieces. "Just so you know, I've already got my lawyer on the case, and I'll bet she's scarier than yours. If I want to sneak money to you on the sly, it'll be done before you know it's happening and there'll be nothing you can do about it."

"Now you see, that's your inner superhero waving his flag. You think you're saving a damsel in distress, but I promise you, I'm not in distress."

"Have you thought that maybe this isn't about you, it's about me? How do you know I'm not the one buying a baby?"

"What? No!"

"And if I told you straight out that I am?"

"I guess I'd ask why you chose me."

Their eyes met. Held. Something flashed inside him. Hot. Vivid. "And I'd answer…*because* it's you," he said. And the instant the words were out, he knew they were true. He was doing this not only *for* her, but because it *was* her. Because she was the one pure thing in his life and he needed her and if they shared a child he'd always have her. And his child…? Well, of course he had more to offer his child than money: he had *her*. Her light, to cancel out his darkness.

"Oh!" she said, blinking furiously.

Shit! "Don't go troll on me," he warned.

"I won't. I promise. It's just…nice. To hear that."

"Yeah, well, don't get sentimental about it. It's to my benefit to give my kid a good mother. Less chance it'll want to come and live with me one day."

"Oh!" she said again, and gave a tiny sniff that freaked him out.

"Jesus, Romy! Get a grip. Are you on hormones or something?"

"No. No, no, that's just nice to hear, too. In a…a twisted kind of way."

"That's me—twisted."

She gave him that peer-into-your-brain look again. "Why do you always do that, Matt?"

"What?"

"Make yourself something…less."

He hunched a shoulder. "I'm not doing anything except reminding you there's something in this for both of us. Right, we still have a hundred documents to get through and I'll be ripping up any that have a tear splotch on them, so get it together."

She wiped a finger under each eye. "It's not a hundred, it's fifteen."

"That's my girl! Precision document preparer." He laughed. "We'll get through a paltry fifteen like a hot knife through butter."

He hoped she'd laugh, too, but she didn't. She was watching him, her forehead creased as though she wasn't sure whether or not she should be frowning, and Matt felt panic edge its way up his spine because maybe she was about to call things off—and suddenly, unexpectedly, he knew he'd move heaven and hell to keep the deal alive. "Are we good, Romy?" he asked.

She bit her lip, and he did his best to make himself

look nonthreatening. If he could have willed the right response out of her, he would have—he certainly directed every synapse in his brain at her as he silently urged: *Say yes...say yes...say yes, damn you.*

"Yes," she said, and his limbs went weak with relief. "Yes, we're good."

"So," he said, as nonchalantly as he could manage. "What's next?"

She flipped a page, another, another, muttering something under her breath. He knew what she was doing. Sorting the documents, easiest to hardest, building her case. The muttering thing usually made him want to get her in a headlock, rub his knuckles against her scalp and warn her she was talking out loud, not in her head. But not tonight. Tonight, for reasons he *did not want to face*, it made him want to take her on his lap like he used to do at college when something was worrying her. But this was different from college. Because he didn't just want to reassure her, he wanted to kiss her.

He forced his eyes away from her mouth to her hands, and the platinum signet ring on her right pinky finger caught his eye. She'd worn it every day since Teague had given it to her for her twenty-first birthday seven years ago, and he barely noticed it anymore. But now he wanted to rip it off her finger and throw it into the fire. What a fucking crazy upended night this was turning out to be.

"This one," she said, and picked out a page.

The ring caught the overhead light, distracting him. "Huh?"

She held the page out to him. "Timing."

He ignored the page. He wanted this done. Wrapped

up. Settled, before she could change her mind. "Choose any time you want—I'll fit in with you. Next."

Flip. Shuffle. She held out another page. "Clinic options in San Francisco."

He ignored that document, too. "Mark your preferred one and I'll make an appointment. Next."

New page—held out. "The process."

"Fuck, Romy. I grab a girlie magazine and jack off. Do you really think I need instructions? Next."

She chose a new page, held it out to him, then pulled it back and put it on top of the pile. "You know what?" she said, neatening the edges of her documents as that fucking ring flash-flash-flashed at him. "Let's stop pretending you're interested in the paperwork. Just point me in the direction of the kitchen so I can make your *fucking* paella! And *then*, since your mind is clearly on what time Camilla's arriving and not on me, set the table for the two of you, *not* all three of us, and I'll go back to my hotel, and that way—"

She broke off as his hand shot across the desk and latched itself around her right wrist, shocking the bejesus out of both of them. He watched her fingers curl, then flex, then curl again—but she didn't break his hold the way she should have if she had any sense. He imagined her feeling the tremor that was shimmering through him and working out what it meant, then blushing for him the way she had for Lennie. Her slumberous eyes half closing as she offered herself to him. He could see her on the desktop, raising the skirt of her cherry-red dress...see himself taking off her black stockings, sliding her panties down her legs. One lick, to taste her. *Do that again, Matt...lick me... I want you to do everything to me...anything you want...*

"Matt," she said, in that same breathy whisper she'd used when he'd hugged her too hard in the entrance hall, and he released her just as suddenly as he had then. He had to get his shit together. Stop the Jekyll and Hyde fuckery.

He put his hands palm down on the desk, ordered them to stay there. Splayed his fingers, then brought them in again, splayed…and back. Breathing, breathing, breathing through the moment of holy-hell panic and trying to remember the last thing she'd said and how he was supposed to respond. Something about the documents…kitchen…paella…Camilla…

"Why would you think Camilla was coming for dinner?"

"Because your girlfriends always do."

"Point of clarification, Romy—I haven't had a 'girlfriend' since I was seventeen."

"Well, *whatever* you call them, they're always joining us for dinner or lunch or drinks or something."

"I *call* them by their name."

"You know what I mean."

"Hookups, then. I call them hookups."

"I'm talking about women who are *more* than casual hookups."

"They're *all* casual hookups."

"Um…no! You met Camilla a week before Thanksgiving, and I called you two weeks ago—five weeks *after* Thanksgiving—and you were still with her. That length of time with someone does *not* equal a casual hookup."

"What would you call it?"

"An affair, maybe?"

"Affair? Fuck!"

"What's wrong with *affair*?"

"*Affair* is so *bourgeois*," he said, and immediately recognized *bourgeois* as one of his father's words. *Why be bourgeois, Matthew, when you can be bohemian?* How many times had he heard variations on that theme? And now he was parroting his father to Romy! What the hell was wrong with him tonight?

"Well, how *'bourgeois'* is it to answer a guy's phone for him?" Romy asked. "Casual hookups don't answer your phone."

"Yeah, well, she was on top, it was easier for her to reach it," he said, goaded by who-knew-what into yet more assholery.

Her eyes went wide. "You spoke to me in the middle of having *sex* with her? You—you—"

"Bastard? Is that the word you're looking for? Because *that's* bourgeois." Her eyes were still wide, and her naïveté provoked him into wanting to shock her further. Shock her…show her who she was dealing with here. "It's just sex, Romy, and nonexclusive at that. *Hookup* fits better than *affair*, trust me on this. And since Camilla hasn't called me since that night, whatever she *was*, she's not *it* anymore."

"Not exclusive?" Pause. "You mean exclusive as in—"

"Monogamous."

"You were hooking up with other women simultaneously?"

"Not at *exactly* the same time, if you know what I mean."

"Well, that's…something. I guess."

"Although I have in the past. There's nothing quite like a threesome."

"Oh," she said faintly, "I see. But…but not with Camilla. But doesn't that mean—?"

"Camilla, of course, was hooking up with other men—she's not at all bourgeois."

"I see."

"Good," he said. "Now you know."

"I just thought…"

"What? That I was an innocent, clean-cut boy?"

"I thought…at least you used to be… I was *sure* you were…monogamous."

"Still am, on request. You want monogamy, you got it. That tends to get the cardinal rule broken a little faster, though, and that's always the end," he said, threading his voice with amusement.

"Cardinal rule? How do I not know about a cardinal rule after ten years?"

"You don't know because you don't break it, Romy. You don't *say* it."

"Say *what*, Matthew?"

"That you love me."

Romy had this thing she did when she was trying to make sense of something that did not compute: a raised-eyebrow blink in slow motion, which he called her blink of insanity. She did it now. "A woman tells you she loves you, your instant reaction is to *dump* her?"

"I don't like the word *dump*. It's more what I'd call a withdrawal of interest."

"Now, you see, I think a woman might still regard that as being dumped."

"Then she'd be wrong, because dumping implies there was a relationship. And, like I said, I haven't had one of those since I was—"

"Seventeen? She must have been some girl, the one you were with at seventeen, to be so hard to replace."

"Oh, yes, Gail was some girl, all right," Matt said, and although his voice was steady, the old sick rage he thought he was done with welled up in him.

Romy saw it, too. Or sensed it. He could tell. Ah shit. He braced for follow-on questions, holding his breath as she did the open-shut mouth routine...

But she must have decided that was one story too many, because with a slight shake of her head, she changed tack. "So when you *are* monogamous," she said, "they fall in love...when? Are we talking days? Weeks? Months?"

He managed an almost-natural laugh. "You think I keep track?"

"Too many to keep track of? Maybe you and Artie could invent a track-keeping app."

"Smart-ass."

Pause. "So...how long does it take *you* to fall in love, Matt?"

"What is this? The Spanish Inquisition?" He tried out another laugh, but this one missed natural by a mile.

"Just a simple question."

"Then here's a simple answer—I don't."

"Not since you were seventeen, I suppose."

Back to that. He pushed his chair back from the desk, then pulled it straight back in. Restless. Agitated. "It's like this: both people in a...a..."

"Relationship?"

"...*situation* need to want the same thing or someone's going to get hurt."

"Are you saying you never want the same thing they do?"

"No, sometimes we want *exactly* the same thing, and that's great."

"But it's never love?"

"Search your memory for a contradictory example, Romy. You won't find one."

"Well, that's a shame, because you've gone out with a lot of wonderful women." She sighed. "I hope you at least warn them up front what to expect."

"Oh, I make it clear, what's in it for both of us."

"Sex."

"*Good* sex. And fun. And respect. I'm not jealous or possessive, which means they can leave whenever they like, no questions asked. No stalking or bad-mouthing or revenge porn when it's over. Friendship if they're up for that at the end, although very few are and that's okay, too. I just...don't want them to love me."

"And yet they *do* love you, Matt. I've talked enough of them off the ledge at the end to know it."

He shook his head, dismissive. "They don't stay on the ledge for long. And that's because although they *say* they love me, they really don't."

"You can't know that."

"I know they almost invariably speak those magic words at the peak of an orgasm, which tells me it's about sex. And if they think sex is the way to my heart, they sure as fuck don't know me well enough to love me. In fact, I'll let you in on a deep dark secret about the way to my heart, Romy." He leaned across the desk, confidante-style, and lowered his voice. "There *is* no way, because I don't *have* a heart."

"If that were true I wouldn't have trusted you all these years and I wouldn't be here now. I trust you, Matt. I trust you absolutely."

"Trust in anything you like except my heart. Or my soul, come to think of it. I definitely don't have one of those. It's the Carter curse, inherited along with the hair. So don't look into my eyes for too long or I'll steal yours." He leaned back in his chair and smiled mockingly. "Have you thought what'll happen if you have a red-haired, soul-stealing kid? Will you reject the baby?"

She looked directly into his eyes. "I like your red hair. I want the baby to have it."

That look, so serious and compelling, was like a blow to the chest, and it took Matt a moment to absorb the impact. Trust, she'd said she trusted him. And it was in her eyes. Even after everything he'd just told her. She was a babe in the woods, wandering through the forest in her red dress with no idea wolves were lurking behind the trees. She needed to be protected from the likes of him.

"Yeah well, I suggest you look past the red hair," he said, "and understand that the only thing I have to offer is a very big cock."

She surprised him by not flinching, by looking at him just as steadily, as seriously, as trustingly. "And if I were to say that I *love* your red hair? That I love *everything* about you? What would you do, Matthew? Would you dump me? And...and Veronica and Rafael and Artie and Teague? Would you dump them, too? Because I— they—*we*—all love you! How could we not, when you push and pull us to do things we never would otherwise? The baby you're giving me, for starters."

"I told you—that's for me."

"Then what about the time I couldn't afford the airfare to Sydney for Frankie's wedding, and lo and behold, a ticket materialized."

"Air miles—it cost me nothing!"

"And Artie—the software that would have stayed in your heads if not for you. You made him rich."

"Made me rich, too, and it wouldn't have happened without his brain."

"Then what about the Silicon Valley tech hub you set up and dragged him into."

"That's a partnership, benefiting me, too."

"You pushed Rafael into entering that international writing competition, which he won."

"He didn't take much pushing."

"You got Veronica the gig with the university's Student Healthcare Outreach program because she needed a good deed on her CV."

"Stop!"

"And Teague only snagged a spot crewing in the Sydney Hobart Yacht Race because of you."

"Teague almost drowned!"

"He loved every minute of it! And he loves *you*. Like a brother. He's told me so."

"Goddammit, Romy." He looked away from her, because that shook him. Teague. *Teague*, who'd seen more than the others, who'd guessed it all, who fucking *knew*. Teague might be the closest anyone had come to sainthood, but he wasn't stupid enough to want a brother like Matt. Romy was deluding herself. He brought his eyes back to her. "You're wrong. All those things…they're nothing. I've done other stuff you wouldn't congratulate me for, believe me."

"What stuff?"

He had to force himself not to look away again; to do so once was barely acceptable; twice would give too much away. "Stuff you don't need to know."

"Why can't I know?"

"Because you'd back out of this deal if you did."

For a long moment she just looked at him. And then she sighed. "How am I supposed to understand why it's so hard to accept that people love you if you won't tell me?"

"You don't have to understand, you only have to accept that to me, love is nothing but an overused word," he said. "I love ice cream, oysters, pizza. I love cooking, sailing, camping. How's anyone supposed to take that word seriously when it's thrown out about anything and everything? So I'm asking you not to say it, the way you haven't said it for ten years."

"I *must* have said it before."

"Not to me. And I figure if you were ever going to say it, you'd have said it by now. I don't *want* to hear it, Romy, so don't say it now." He stopped to take a calming breath. "There are other words for what we have. More meaningful words. Words that can't be desecrated. Words like *friendship*, *camaraderie*, *affection*. Be as creative as you want. Just don't call it love."

"Okay." She held up her hands, palms out, surrender. "This is me not calling it love."

"Good."

"I hereby promise not to love you."

"Great."

"I refuse to love you."

"Okay, I get it, Romy, give it a rest."

"It's not like I was going to propose marriage."

"Fucking fantastic. Go you. Now, moving *on*!"

She snatched up the page on top of her pile. "Visitation," she announced. "My lawyer thinks—"

"Not interested in anything your lawyer says," Matt

interrupted irritably. "I'll just tell you what I want—access without restrictions when I'm in London."

"I'm sure we can come up with a form of words to that effect," she said, all business now. "You're only in London for one week a year, so give me advance notice and I'll make sure I'm not out of town."

"It'll be more than once a year. I'll be over in four months' time to look at premises, and then again two months after that to sort out tenancy agreements."

"Premises? What have I missed?"

"Artie and I are opening a tech start-up hub in London similar to the Silicon Valley one. He's taking the lead so he's already over there, but once it's up and running, I'll be there on and off for the first year at least."

"Okay. No problem. Like I said, advance notice, and I'll make it easy for you to see the baby." She shot him a curious look. "If that's really what you want."

"Why wouldn't I want it?"

"You indicated on the phone you were looking for a no-strings godfather role. It's a little…confusing, I guess, to hear you talk about unrestricted access. And I…I just think it's a good idea to start as you mean to go on."

"What does *that* mean?"

"That you don't keep changing your mind—like, one year you decide to come every month, the next year you come once in the whole year. Children need certainty."

"Okay then, how about we leave it at once a year, scheduled, and you decide whether or not to allow other visits on a rolling basis."

"Fine. Then let's move on to—"

"I'm not finished."

She waited, watching him warily.

"The kid's going to be half-American," he went on,

"so if I'm only going to be guaranteed one visit a year, you need to bring it out here once a year. For…I don't know…heritage purposes."

"Easy! I'm already here once a year—and I'll be over more often if I land Suzanne Plieu as a client. She's keen to open a fine dining restaurant in New York and we've had a preliminary chat about what I can do to help her find a partner."

"New York is Teague's territory, not mine."

"Well, yeees." That same curious look, as though she were trying to work him out. "And if Suzanne needs a lawyer, he'd be—"

"I'm not talking about Suzanne's restaurants or legal needs. I'm talking about you being needed in San Francisco with me, the kid's father, not in New York with Teague."

"It's going to depend on whether I can afford it."

"*I* can afford it."

"My clients pay for my travel here and you're not my client."

"Then start working on your aversion to staying with me. No accommodation costs, and I won't *feel* like your client when you sashay in with your briefcase."

"I can't stay with you, Matt."

"Why not? You stay with Teague when you're in New York."

"Only when my work is finished."

"Should I point out that you're not working tonight?"

Pause. He knew that slight twist to her mouth. She was working out what to say. "Teague's apartment is… spacious. It's easier there."

"And I now have a large house. So when you come

with the kid, you stay. As long as your 'form of words' contains that, we're good."

"We're not good in that case."

"Why not?"

And she was up, out of her chair, walking over to the fireplace, dragging her hands through her hair—which she never, ever did.

"Why not?" he asked again, when she just stood there looking into the flames.

"It won't work."

"Asking again—why not?"

Shake of her head.

"Romy, what's going on? Why did I buy a house with a million rooms if you and the kid are going to stay in a hotel?"

She turned to face him then. "But th-that's not why you bought the house!"

"Isn't it?"

He saw the breath she took, and prepared himself for an argument.

"Okay then, Matthew," she said, "in the spirit of ne-gotiation—"

"It's not negotiable."

"—I'll *agree* to stay here, on the condition that I know in advance who else will be here and I can opt out if I'm uncomfortable."

"Uncomfortable?"

"I don't want to impinge on your lifestyle."

"My 'lifestyle'?"

"There'll be times it won't be appropriate for me to stay, depending on...on who..."

He shot to his feet. "Who I'm *fucking*? Is that what

you mean?" He realized he'd yelled that, but couldn't get the anger under control enough to care.

"If you'd let me expl—"

"You think I'm going to have someone stashed in my bedroom for after I've finished reading my kid a bedtime story?" Yelled again.

"I wouldn't put it quite like—"

"Will I have to fill out a form? Name, age, occupation, social security number? Nominate what nights of the week I intend to fuck them?"

"Oh, for God's sake!" she said, firing up at last and yelling back at him. "I already *know* what nights of the week! *Every* damn night of *every* damn week! That's the problem!"

"I'm glad you appreciate my stamina!"

"That place we shared back in the day had paper-thin walls! We *all* appreciated your stamina! Veronica and I used to joke about buying shares in Durex, you went through so many jumbo boxes of condoms!"

"So you counted my condoms and listened in? Interesting."

"Sadly, the pillow I jammed over my head to filter out the moans, grunts and squeals didn't quite block everything."

"What can I say? I do a good job. A better job than Teague, now I think of it, since he didn't ever stay with you overnight."

"This isn't about Teague."

"No, it isn't, is it, or maybe *I* would have heard something."

"Not over the racket going on in *your* room!"

"Jealous?"

She raised her chin. "Just over it! Okay? I'm over it!

I don't *want* to hear you anymore! I've had *enough* of hearing you!" And she was on the move again, storming over to the drapes, trying to drag them open as though their very existence was cutting off her oxygen supply.

He stalked across the room, reached her, spun her. "Then how about you stay tonight and test the sound-proofing? In the absence of my usual fuck noises you can listen for the loud howl of sexual frustration that'll be coming out of my room because I haven't had sex for two fucking *weeks*! Does that scare you, Romy?"

"Why should it scare me?"

"Because you're here alone with me and I…I… Arrrggh! It's dangerous, can't you see that?"

"Dangerous how?"

"Jesus, Romy, how naive *are* you?" Matt said. The room was hot, stifling, claustrophobic. He needed air, needed…*something*! "Fuck this!" He reached past her, grabbed a handful of velvet, yanked on it, heard a satisfying rip, and then the drapes dropped to the floor. He kicked them for good measure. "When are you going to accept that I'm not your damn hero, Romy? I'm not like Teague. I don't *do* chastity, and yet I've just told you I *have* done it, for *two weeks*."

"So *what*?"

"So I'm a *sex addict*. And you're *here*."

"A sex addict would have made a move on me the night we met! God knows I gave you the chance! So don't talk to me about not 'doing' chastity when you've been nothing *but* chaste with me for ten years!"

"You're not like the others!"

"Well, that just goes to show that you're an *idiot*! Because I *am* like the others. I'm *exactly* like the others. I want what *they* want, damn you!"

Sudden, charged silence.

Matt's skin prickled, his senses going on high alert. "Tell me what you mean," he said, breathing the words. "What you want."

She closed her eyes. Heartbeat. Opened them. "You know what I mean. You of all men *know* what women mean!" And it was as though the angry energy drained out of her, even though her hands had clenched into fists by her sides. "What I want is you. I want…you."

CHAPTER THREE

TEN YEARS OF not saying the words, and now they were out, hanging between them.

Romy's heart was beating hard enough to leap out of her body. And Matt looked rigid enough to bounce the poor thing off his chest. Like a stone column. Or... or petrified wood.

Petrified being the operative word.

She choked down a rising bubble of hysterical laughter at the notion that big, bad Matt could be scared of her. *She* was the one who should be scared. Scared he'd tell her no and leave her with nothing: friendship in tatters, no baby and still no clue about what it was like to...to *be* with him like all those other women.

"You don't know what you're saying," Matt said.

And on the spot, she consigned any last vestige of caution to hell. For ten long years she'd been subjugating her lust for him. That was long enough! "Yes, Matt, I do," she said. "Exactly what I *did* say. I want you. But you can call it Plan B if that's easier for you to deal with."

"Plan B?"

"I need to get pregnant. You offered to provide the sperm. We've discussed the turkey baster method—

Plan A—but there's no reason it can't be done the old-fashioned way—Plan B."

"Old-fashioned way."

"We have a window of opportunity here. It's almost like fate stepped in."

"Window of opportunity," he said, like he was having trouble keeping up.

"Neither of us has someone in our lives—a minor miracle in your case. You said you were sexually frustrated, so you need a release valve, and here I am offering to be it."

"Release valve."

"From my perspective, it's cheaper than IVF. It's certainly more *efficient*. Like a direct deposit, cutting out the middleman."

"Direct deposit."

"Oh, for God's sake, stop repeating everything I say," she semiexploded as her resolve frayed around the edges. "It's easy to understand, isn't it? It's just a one-night stand! We've already been through your ground rules about not mistaking sex for anything more, so don't worry that I'll be expecting a bourgeois romance. And you're not the only one who knows what it is to be sexually frustrated, because it's been a while for me, let me tell you, and I daresay it'll be a much *longer* while once I'm pregnant."

"One-night stand."

"Yes, one night. No encore required. If it doesn't work, we simply revert to the turkey baster/courier option and…and…and aren't you going to say something?"

"No encore."

"Something that's *not* a stupid repeat of what I've already said."

She waited; he stared.

Romy couldn't recall an instance in which Matt had taken this long to make a decision. She wondered if she should shorthand the argument by taking off her dress.

"Matt…" she said, reaching for the zipper at her left side—but before she could touch it, a log fell in the fireplace, jolting the momentum out of her so that she lost her nerve. "Forget it. It was just a suggestion. If you can't bring yourself to do it, there's nothing more to be said. Plan A it is."

"I'm pretty sure I can bring myself to do it," he said, and then he started laughing as though she'd told the funniest joke on the world.

She drew herself up, glaring at him. "I'm glad I've managed to amuse you."

She tried to push past him, but he blocked her. "Wait!" he said.

"We've wasted enough time. We need to go back to the paperwork."

Again he blocked her. "I said wait. Let's at least *talk* about Plan B."

"I'm no longer interested in Plan B."

"Why not?"

"Because you've just reminded me how it ends."

"How can that be when it hasn't happened yet?"

"It'll be a carbon copy of the time I told you Jeff Blewett kissed like his mouth was an octopus suction cup and you dared me to let you demonstrate the way you imagined that to be. I was stupid enough to say yes because I thought…I thought…never mind what I thought, it doesn't *matter* what I thought, because at the last minute you changed direction and gave me a hickey right here…" jabbing at the center of her forehead "…and no amount of makeup would cover it up so I went around for two days looking like I'd been hit by a cricket ball and you thought it was all hilarious."

"So how about I try it now?"

"I don't need another forehead hickey, thank you."

"I mean I could kiss you for real. And then…well, then you could decide if we go ahead with Plan B."

"It'd serve you right if I said yes."

"So say it."

Romy licked her lips nervously. "Be careful, Matt, or I really will call your bluff."

"Call it. I dare you to."

"After the forehead hickey, you're going to have to convince me you'll be able to get it up at the crucial moment before I go any further," she said.

He took a step back from her, which she didn't consider promising. "One look at me will tell you that's not going to be a problem. So go on and look."

She examined his face, trying to gauge his seriousness. She was so keyed up, she'd rip his throat out if she saw so much as a glint of humor in his eye.

"Lower," he instructed.

Her eyes dropped to his chest.

"Jesus, Romy, are you doing this on purpose? Lower!"

To his jeans. "Oh."

"Bingo," he said.

She raised her eyes to his face again. "I've heard that's always there."

"Are you fucking nuts? I'd never function as a human being if that were the case." He reached for her then. "But it's been there since you walked in tonight." Folded her into his arms. "So if you're telling me you didn't feel it in the entrance hall, I'm going to think I've shrunk.

And I know I'm ten years past my sexual peak, but it seemed to work very…*sizably*, shall we say, two weeks ago."

She choked on a laugh. "Your ego is gargantuan."

"My ego isn't the thing that's gargantuan. Although if you really didn't notice the size of my cock when you first arrived, it's going to need some stroking."

"I hope you mean your ego."

"Actually, I really do mean my cock. So stay riiight… theeere, ahhhhh, that feels good." Nudging his cock against her. "Think about what it means vis-à-vis your question about whether or not I can bring myself to do it."

"What it means…" she breathed out, fairly sure she could orgasm just from what he was doing here and now.

"It means yes I can, and when I do it's going to be amazing. I'll make it amazing for you, Romy. The moment you say yes."

Same man she'd been friends with for ten years, same man who'd hugged her, tousled her hair, dragged her onto his lap, forced her earrings through her ill-pierced left earlobe. But this was different. *He* was different. And she had a premonition that he would always be different, from this moment.

The fear of losing him if she said the "yes" he was asking for was real, because women in whom Matt had a sexual interest were never around for long. The only women who lasted in his life were those who dated his friends—like Veronica, whom he treated like a sister even after her split from Rafael. And wasn't that at least one reason Romy had transferred her starry eyes from Matt to Teague in their freshman year? Not only because Teague really was perfect but because Matt had *brought* him to her, thereby marking her place in Matt's life while she got her head around consigning Matt to the friend zone?

How long would she last if she stepped out of that zone? Matt had said friendship at the end was possible with women he'd had sex with but that most didn't want it. Why would she be any different from all those other women?

The baby, of course. The baby made her different. But the baby made her vulnerable, too, because it was precious not only for its own sake but because it would be a part of Matt that would always belong to her, a part she was allowed to love. She so wanted to believe Matt would come to love the baby, which would be like loving a part of her, even if he didn't call it love.

Impossible to risk all that for one night…and yet just as impossible *not* to after wanting him for so long. Oh, how she wished she could blur the line between sex and friendship instead of stepping over it, keeping everything in its proper place.

If the sex was awful, she probably could. They'd laughingly accept that they'd given it the old college try and there was no harm done whether she was pregnant— experiment concluded successfully—or not—back to Plan A.

If it was awful…

But Romy knew it wouldn't be awful.

The tightness of her skin told her that. Her racing heart, too. The way the smell of his pine-tree-scented soap made her want to lick him.

Those were the feelings lovers had, not friends.

Lovers.

Love.

Don't call it love. Call it anything *except* love. Friendship, camaraderie, affection. A window of opportunity. A cheaper, faster, more efficient method of sperm insertion. Release valve. Direct deposit. Plan B. Sex, just sex.

If she kept all those descriptions in mind, surely she could do this. She could blur the line, she *would* blur the line, and she'd survive the end.

"All right, yes," she breathed, both brave and terrified.

He pulled her in even more tightly. "Then I suggest we go upstairs immediately because it's not your forehead I want to suck right now, and if we don't move, I'm afraid I'll drag you down to the floor and have my evil way with you right here."

She huffed out a desperate laugh. "Evil is fine by me."

He rubbed his cheek across the top of her head, and she felt him sigh even though she didn't hear it. "Careful what you say, Romy."

CHAPTER FOUR

ROMY MADE IT to the entrance hall—and stopped.

"The stairs on the left." Matt, behind her.

She hesitated. "Do you really think we can be friends at the end of this?" she asked.

"That's the idea."

"It didn't work out that way for Veronica and Rafael. They haven't spoken to each other since graduation."

"Those two weren't friends to start with, Romy. They were a Molotov cocktail from the night we all met, hell-bent on being in love. But you and I are a whole different ball game. We've got our plan straight."

"Plan B," she said. What a time to realize that for once in her life she didn't *really* have a plan—not for the mechanics of what would happen next. She was far from having an encyclopedic knowledge of the *Kama Sutra*—whereas Matt, whose sexual prowess was the stuff of legend, probably had his own annotated version.

"What is it?" he asked.

"Nothing," she said in a small voice.

Pause. "Do you want to stop?"

"No." Same tiny voice.

"Because if you've changed your mind, this would be a good time to tell me."

"I haven't changed my mind," she said, and made it to the base of the stairs before stopping again. Oh God, what if she couldn't even get him to have an orgasm and he ended up just as sexually frustrated at the end as he'd been at the beginning?

Matt's hands landed on her hips. She expected him to urge her to go up, but instead he pulled her back against him as though they had all the time in the world. She swallowed a mouthful of saliva as she felt his erection prodding against her back. He'd said he had a very big cock and he wasn't kidding. If its size really was illustrative of Matt being ten years past his sexual peak, he must have had the penis of a freaking giant at eighteen.

"Romy?" he said, with a tingle-inducing nudge at her ear. "Be certain you want this, because there'll come a point when I'll stop asking and you'll have to *tell* me if something's bothering you."

"There's no problem," she lied—because she wasn't going to ask him if he'd ever been bored enough to fall asleep halfway through sex—and headed up the stairs, only to stop again at the top.

Matt must have reached that point where he stopped asking, because all he said was, "To the left, fourth door, the open one."

Inhale, step, exhale, step, inhale, step, exhale.

Just the feel of his hands on her hips was making her lust for him in a way she'd never thought possible. What would she do for him when his hands were on her naked flesh? Anything, she suspected. Anything at all. Everything he asked.

Now breathe. Because they'd reached the bedroom. The final frontier.

She stepped over the threshold. Dark floorboards,

white walls, a night view of San Francisco Bay in the distance, through curtains opened wide. There was an inner door she assumed led through to a bathroom. Aside from a built-in wardrobe, the only furniture was a gigantic bed and one armchair—a scarcity that amplified the room's size.

"It's big," she said.

"So all the girls say."

And somehow, that made her laugh as she turned to face him, despite her anxiety. "Are you obsessed with size?"

"Only with what I can do with it."

"Don't overpromise, Matthew."

"Not an overpromise," he said huskily, and ran his hand over her hair—a sensual stroke that made her breath catch in her throat. "Are you nervous, Romy?"

"No," she said—but a tic jumped to life at the side of her mouth and gave the lie to that. "Not…really."

Matt pressed his thumb over the tic. "We'll take it as slowly as we need to. I'm not going to do anything I think you won't like, I promise. Stop me anytime. I won't be angry. I won't argue. I won't pressure you. We'll just find another way."

She gestured to the bed, so nervous she could barely stand. "Why don't you tell me what position you want me in so we can get started?"

"Romy! We're not even naked yet."

"I'd rather have it worked out in my head before we take our clothes off so we don't get…you know… distracted."

"Getting…you know…distracted is kind of the aim. So why don't we just play it by ear?"

"By ear?" She reached up and touched her left earlobe, the one he'd nudged with his nose, feeling a residual tingle. "No, that won't work."

He looked at her for a long, quiet moment. "If you don't want to touch me, Romy, there's no point to this."

"I do want to. But I...I just know I could prepare myself better if I knew where we were headed."

"You're overthinking it."

"But what if I suck?"

"Then that'll be perfect."

"Oh!" She laughed. "You know what I mean."

He sighed. "I want you, Romy. I *want* you, *however* this unfolds. I'm telling you that straight. And you know how important you are to me outside this room, which means I have to know this is what you really want. So tell me. Tell me you want me."

"I already t-told you."

"Tell me again. Make me believe it. Or this stops now."

Her pulse leaped—fear, excitement. "I want you."

"Tell me you want me to not only make you pregnant, but to make you come."

Another leap. "Oh God."

"Tell me."

"Fine. I want you to make me come, and come, and come." She rolled her eyes at him. "There. I said it. Now can we get on with it?"

"Come and come and *come*," he repeated.

"Well...yes."

He smiled. "Pfft."

"Pfft?"

"Three orgasms is for amateurs. Let's make it four." He turned her to face the bed. "You want to talk positions? This is how I want you. Go and lie facedown across the bed with your hips at the edge."

Her hands went to her zipper. "Should I—?"

"Leave your clothes on. We'll do this first orgasm fast so you can relax."

Romy went to the bed and took up the position Matt had instructed her to take, her heartbeat now at a gallop. Oh God. Oh God, oh God, oh God, this was going to happen, it really, really was. She was about to find out why all those girls had followed him all over campus, why so many women since had put their lives on hold waiting for him to come back to them even though history told them he'd never do it. She'd know the secret to being the one for him, and she didn't *care* that it was only for one night, she *wouldn't* care, wouldn't stop to think, wouldn't stop at all. She'd waited too long for this.

"And don't worry, you don't have to prepare yourself," he said, coming up behind her, "because *I'm* going to prepare you."

Next second, he was easing her slightly backward and opening her legs. She felt a rush of moisture between her thighs, readying her for what would come next.

"Good," Matt said, as though he'd seen that gush, and Romy *wanted* him to see it, wanted him to *feel* it, wanted him to taste it. The anticipation was already better than anything she'd actually experienced.

He raised the skirt of her dress, hissed in a breath, slid his hands around the bands of those black socks that suddenly seemed erotic rather than fashionable. "These stay on," he said huskily.

"Whatever you want."

"You have no idea how much I wish…"

"You wish…?" she breathed, doing some wishing of her own—that he'd finish what he'd been about to say so she could tell him yes, do it, do anything, do everything; it was one night and she wanted it all.

But he didn't complete the sentence. Instead he moved his hands to the bare flesh of her upper thighs above her socks, and Romy lost interest in anything but his stroking fingers.

"You are so absolutely perfect," he said, his voice a raw note off an actual throb. "Now open your legs a little more." She obeyed, only to be told, "Wider, I need room to kneel behind you so I can get my tongue in."

Tongue. She started to tremble, and bit at her bottom lip, determined not to moan. *Tongue.* God help her, she was going to come the moment he touched it to her. She gripped two handfuls of his duvet in preparation.

"Ordinarily I'd suck you through your panties before taking them off," he said, causing another gush. It was a reflex action, to close her legs and contain it, but he laughed, low and strained, and said, "Oh no, you don't," and pushed her thighs wider apart. "But I want my tongue right on you, so I think…yes, I think I'll leave those snug panties of yours on and just move them…" sliding his fingers under the crotch "…so I can see them as I lick you. Win-win for me."

He grazed her with his fingers, only *just* touching her, making her gasp before she could catch it back. Then one quick tug, and Matt hissed in another breath, groaned this one back out. How did she look from back there, with the soaking-wet crotch of her lilac panties shoved aside? What was he thinking, seeing her like that—half on display, half hidden, swollen with need? Ah God, who cared what she looked like or what he thought, as long as he touched her.

"So pretty—more than I could have imagined," Matt

said, and next second he was kneeling between her open thighs. "Better than I deserve." That was added so softly, her heart thumping so strongly, Romy wasn't sure she'd heard him correctly. It didn't make sense, that he could not deserve her. Not when she was so sure she didn't deserve *him*, when she'd somehow tricked him into this.

"Wh-what?" she asked, but his answer was to tug the crotch of her panties still farther aside.

His answer was to lick all the way along her sex with the flat of his tongue so that she jerked and cried out, her hands twisting in the duvet, her leg muscles quivering, and she cared about nothing except that he keep going. He licked her again, and again and again, until she was pushing herself against his mouth. *Harder, harder.* She screamed it only in her head, but it was as though Matt heard her, because he settled into a rhythm, directing his assault at her clitoris now, alternating the flat of his tongue with the tip. Strokes and flicks, changing the pressure from hard to soft and back, increasing speed. Faster, faster, faster. It was coming, she could feel it, she didn't even have to reach for it, didn't have to will it. She had no control. One, two, three harder licks, and he sucked her clit into his mouth. He kept sucking until she was ready to bang her head on the mattress, so great was the effort it took not to humiliate herself by begging him to finish it. Her breaths were ragged, hips thrusting convulsively back and forth as though he were actually fucking her and she was meeting each lunge of his cock, but his mouth stayed with her, winding her tight like a key in a toy. *His* toy.

Something had to give. Something had to break. Something had to—

"OooohhhhhmyyyyyGoooooooood." The cry wailed

out of her as the orgasm slammed into her, crashed over her, zigzagged through her like burning, bright, hot lightning.

Matt had to know she was coming, she was rigid with it, pulsing under his mouth, but he didn't stop. He kept tonguing her, going at her until her twitching body went limp. She was still gasping for air as he slowed and finished with one opulent lick. And then…hold, hold, hold, his fingers still on the panties he'd dragged out of his way. He was looking at her, she knew he was, and she had neither the strength nor the desire to stop him. His labored breathing, rough and fast, made her long to know what he was thinking.

But one more lick, a quick kiss, and his thinking was over. He turned brisk, repositioning the crotch of her panties, pulling her dress down to cover her, standing.

"Two minutes and twenty seconds," he said. "Was that fast enough for you, Romy?"

His words settled into her fried brain. Lodged there, stuck there…*stung* there.

She got off the bed, brushed at her dress with an unsteady hand. Saw that he was…smirking? Oh no. No, no, *no*! No smirking allowed. This wasn't going to turn into an octopus hickey moment.

"Yes, that was fast enough," she said briskly, "but that wasn't the deal."

Up went Matt's eyebrows. "I said we'd make the first one fast. You didn't complain."

"About the orgasm, no. But there was no semen, therefore no sperm inserted. So although it was good in terms of elapsed time, it was also a *waste* of time."

"Elapsed time? Wow! How…technical. Okay so I'll be technical back and tell you that happy though I am to oblige your demand for multiple orgasms, men have to pace themselves through four orgasms when they'll only get to two or three for themselves."

"Yes, but in this instance it's not like you need to recharge since that was all about me."

"Nooo, but think about it like...well, like a restaurant meal. Appetizer, main course, dessert, petits fours. Cunnilingus is the appetizer. Good to start with, not going to fill me up."

"But what you just did could have been the petits fours—not everyone gets to them, and they're hardly essential to a satisfying meal."

"Er...you know, I'll try almost anything once, but there's one thing I won't do: drink my own semen. Not going to happen. Hence...appetizer. Gotta get the order right when you're not wearing a condom."

A laugh exploded out of her before she could stop it.

Matt grinned. "I see you understand."

"I'd offer to drink it for you, but it would be a—"

"Waste of sperm. Sad but true. For now, though, you can taste yourself." And he stepped right up to her and cupped her face in his hands.

Why hadn't she ever noticed how big Matt's hands were? How big *he* was, compared to her. She was a woman who liked food and she was no twig—so why did she suddenly *feel* like a twig? Small and snappable. She wanted to fold into him but at the same time pull back, run away, protect herself. Because she was already in danger of wanting more than he was willing to give, and it was hard to remember that whatever was happening now wasn't real. Reality would come roaring back later. Outside this room, outside this moment. When this night out of time was over and they were just friends again.

He tilted her head back so she was looking into his eyes, which had gone dark, the pupils having taken over almost all the green. One of his thumbs moved to her mouth, dragged roughly across her bottom lip. He was going to kiss her. She stiffened, afraid to risk the intimacy of a kiss, wanting to hold herself back from it. She tried to form a phrase with the word *no* in it, one that wouldn't betray her confused sense of truth. But all she could find to say was, "Kissing isn't required." A stupid, mood-shattering thing to say.

"I thought we had a dare going."

"D-dare?"

"Octopus kiss."

"You said you weren't interested in my forehead."

"I'm interested in every part of you."

"If that were true you would have kissed me back then."

"Ah, but if I'd kissed you back then, where would we be now?"

"I think…" she whispered. "I think we'd be nowhere."

"Nowhere…" he repeated, and the way he looked at her was as melancholy as a goodbye, even though they'd barely begun. "I don't like that thought, Romy."

"Neither do I, so let's not think," she said, wanting to take away that look. "Go ahead and kiss me. Do it."

"Forgive me for it first."

"For what?"

"Just…say that you do."

"I'll forgive you anything, always, you know that."

She looked into his eyes as he smoothed his thumbs across her cheeks. And then he gently rested his mouth on hers, and even though he went no further, the moment felt more serious than anything he'd said or done so far. She was balanced on the knife edge of that line she *could not blur*, and one wrong move would slice her in two. Friend...lover. Which was more important to her? Which would Matt choose to be if he couldn't be both? Which would she *want* him to choose?

"Romy," he breathed against her mouth, and she wound her arms around him, held on to him, as though she'd save him from whatever it was that was chasing him. She wished she could pour herself through his skin and comfort him from the inside out, but all she could do was let him take whatever it was he needed from her, the forgiveness she didn't understand.

She knew then there was no choice to be made. She might not know what she'd end up being to him after tonight, but at this moment she would be whatever he wanted her to be.

He tightened his hands on her face and rubbed his mouth across hers, side to side to side, and she catapulted over that damn line into something that was more than friendship and way more than sex.

She parted her lips, inviting him in, expecting a swoop of tongue, a conquest. Instead, he licked at her top lip, then sucked it into his mouth. She opened wider, desperate now for his tongue against hers, and at last he fitted his mouth on hers, tight as a seal. And there it was, his tongue, inside her. Heady, heady moment, the taste of him at last. Unfamiliar—and yet as right as though she'd been expecting exactly this forever. He made a sweep of her mouth, and while her senses were still absorbing the feel of that, he came in hard, his tongue demanding a response from her so that she clung to him and kissed him back, wanting the moment to go on and on.

When he eased away from her and looked down at

her, any hint of gentleness was gone. Something in his eyes she couldn't decipher made her skin prickle all over with heat.

"Orgasm number two coming up, Romy," he said, and there was the promise of something wild in his voice. "And this time, by God, you'll get the sperm."

CHAPTER FIVE

"THAT'S…GOOD," Romy said, and she sounded so breath-
ily gorgeous, Matt wanted to kiss her again.

And maybe he would have, if he didn't have so much
more he wanted to do to her.

It had been so damn *hot* to take her mouth like that,
with the salty, lemony butter from between her thighs
still on his tongue. How had he overlooked the blatant
sensuality of her mouth for so long? He figured it was
because her lips were almost colorless so there was a
hide-in-plain-sight thing going on, but that seemed a
piss-poor excuse now he'd kissed her. Everything about
her mouth was sexy as hell. Wide bottom lip, top lip
almost unnaturally heavy. Lickable. Suckable. If he'd
known how it would be, he'd have kissed her ten years
ago, fuck his good intentions.

And then, of course, they'd be exactly where she said
they'd be: nowhere. Because he'd barely known her, and
he would have turned her into a hookup and it would
have been over within days and he wouldn't have had
the past ten years of having her look at him the way she
always did, like he could slay dragons.

Of course, she had no idea that the biggest dragon in
her life was him. Which was why his conscience kept

tap-tap-tapping at him, telling him that even one night had consequences.

But it was too late to listen to his conscience and so he told himself that since it *was* only one night, the risk was limited. And if he fucked things up…well, hadn't Romy just said she'd forgive him? If she could forgive him anything, surely he could forgive himself for taking this one night. Anyway, he *couldn't* stop now. Not after the way she'd kissed him, like she was making up for those ten lost years. Enticing him to give more, to take more, to devour her mouth, until it was pink and swollen and wet.

Pink, swollen, wet. Like the luscious place between her legs—mysterious, like a dewy flower, its petals closed, peeking out from around the barrier of her panties.

Burrowing his tongue between the petals, searching out every fold, had been an adventure in eroticism. Hidden secrets, buried treasures. And he would use his one night to find every last concealment and plunder it.

How he wished he'd plunged his tongue inside her, but she'd come before he'd had the chance. She was so effortlessly sensitive, it had taken almost no time to get her there. It was like she was made for his mouth. For his cock, too, judging by the way it had throbbed all the way through, demanding its turn. It was a miracle the poor thing hadn't exploded, depositing a gallon of semen through his jeans.

Wasted sperm, Romy would have called that. And so would he. He wanted to be buried all the way inside her when he lost it the first time. And maybe if he was lucky—really, really lucky—the time after that, she might take him into her mouth before she remembered *that* would be a waste of sperm, too. But hell, one suck, one lick, even the briefest kiss, would get him ready to do whatever she wanted. Just the *thought* of seeing her lips wrapped around him was enough to make him wild. It was going to take some willpower to not fall on her like an unrestrained caveman when her clothes came off.

He sent a quick message to his dick: *control yourself.* His dick twitched in response, which Matt interpreted as the penile equivalent of being flipped the bird.

"So…what do you want me to do?" Romy prompted, making him wonder how long he'd been standing there arguing with himself. "Do I take off my clothes now?"

Matt shook his head, closing the small distance between them. "I'll do it," he said, because he needed his first touch to be controlled and once she stripped, all bets would be off. He reached for her zipper. "All you have to do is kick off your shoes."

She kicked. And waited.

He unzipped. And hovered.

Stop, breathe, swallow, control yourself. "Lift your arms," he said.

She did as he asked, and he drew her dress slowly up and off, tossing it in the direction of the chair without taking his eyes from her. He was going to need every ounce of self-restraint he could muster, because he'd never seen a hotter sight than Romy in her underwear. The contrast of the opaque black of her stockings against the matte cream of her upper thighs and the translucent lilac of her panties was pin-up-girl sexy. The neat little patch of brown hair he could see through her panties had his fingers twitching with the need to touch it. Her bra was ivory lace, her full breasts pushing against the cups as though craving both release and his hands, the pastel-pink areolae showing through the material longing to be licked.

"Shall I...?" she asked, reaching behind her for the clasp of her bra.

"No!" Too harsh. *Stop, breathe, control yourself.* "I'll do it." Better. Just.

She nodded, her hands falling to her sides—a simple movement that told him she was ceding herself to him. He liked the idea of her giving her body wholly into his care a little too much for it to be healthy, but he was in thrall to the idea of it nonetheless.

He circled her, drinking in the sight of curves delectably full and lush. He wished he could ravish her a thousand times all at once, in her underwear and out of it. He unclipped her bra, drew the straps down her arms, let it fall to the floor. One long look at her milk-pale back before allowing his eyes to dip lower. When he reached her generous bottom, which was stretching out the lace of her underwear to the limit, he wanted to sink his teeth into her. His hands were shaking as he reached for her panties to push them past her hips, down her legs.

He was glad she wasn't repeating her earlier question about what position he wanted her in; he wasn't sure how he'd frame an answer that included every position known to man. On her back, on her knees, on her side, on top, underneath him, straddling him, sucking him off, on his tongue, in his mouth, hanging from the fucking chandelier. He was past desire; what he felt for her was darker, like a craving—and he knew it was that darkness he had to control at all costs. He *would not* tarnish his bright and brilliant girl.

She stepped out of her panties and he picked them up, sifting them through his eager fingers before throwing them who-the-fuck-knew-where because it struck him that he might savage a hole through the lace—a dead giveaway that he wasn't in control.

He came around in front of her. If she felt uncomfortable wearing nothing but those black stay-ups in front of him, she didn't show it. She looked like she belonged exactly like that, waiting for his touch. Like she trusted him—exactly as she'd said she did—to take care of her.

She reached out a hand, fingertips on his chest, frustratingly tentative. "What about *your* clothes?"

He'd intended to strip off pretty damn quick, but when he looked for outward signs that Romy was as aroused as he was, he got such a shock his hands stopped midaction. Her face was appropriately flushed and her breathing was revealingly fast and shallow—but her nipples were steadfastly flat.

He'd been so busy imagining her breasts with nipples jutting out as per his steamy daydreams in the library, it took him a moment to process that there was no jut. No jut *at all*.

Romy gave a sigh that could only be described as long-suffering. "They're inverted," she explained. "And I'm guessing you haven't seen their like before, despite your revolving bedroom door."

"Inverted. Does that mean…? What does that mean? I mean, I know what *inverted* means but does it…mean…" *Oooooh, shit*. "Does it mean you don't like them to be touched?"

"No! I mean…no."

Thank you, God.

"They're actually super sensitive," she continued, blushing. "It's just not easy to guess how I'm…you know…"

"I know?"

"How I'm...*feeling*, okay?"

God, did she think that was a problem? Because he fucking *loved* the idea of having to work hard to make her show herself. He wanted to work over every inch of her until there was nothing he didn't know. One night. He wanted it all.

He leaned in for a groan of a kiss. "I guess that means I'll have to check how you're *feeling* by doing this..." Sliding his fingers between her thighs to swirl them around her clitoris before slipping them inside her. "Mmm. I think you're almost ready, Romy."

"Not almost. I am. I am ready...I am...I am... ooooh..." she said between pants, and clenched around his fingers as they pulled out of her, as though to keep them inside her. "Oh, please!"

Much as it thrilled Matt that she wanted him to stay there, though, that wasn't the game now. "I *will* please you, Romy, I promise. But first, I want to play with these." His hands went to her breasts, thumbs rubbing over their mysteriously hidden nipples. "Do they ever come out?" he asked, intrigued.

"Sometimes," she said, and arched her back, thrusting her breasts into his hands. "Depending..."

"Depending on what?"

"What you do."

No way was he going to turn down that invitation to experiment!

He pinched around her areolae. "Do you like that?" he asked, and when she groaned and nodded, he said, "Me, too." Only it came out more like a growl, like something feral, so he paused for a moment to rein it all back.

And then he started pinching again, feeling what he couldn't see, the hardness secreted inside. Another buried treasure, waiting to be coaxed out of hiding. Irresistible.

He lowered his head to lick over the top of one nipple, then the other. Her gasping breaths told him she liked that, too, so he kept going. One then the other, back and forth, over and over. She leaned into him, enticing him to more. Her hands were on his hips, gripping hard as he kept licking, experimenting with his tongue. Flat, pointed, lines, circles, hard, soft. What did she like?

The answer was everything, judging by the way she kept shifting from foot to foot, pressing her thighs together, then releasing, then pressing. When he put a hand around each breast and squeezed, narrowing his focal point so he could intensify the pressure of his tongue, she actually moaned. It was hot, hot, *hot*, to hear her. Hot, hot, hot to taste her. He *liked* wanting her like this. The insistent kick of lust, the anticipation of what was to come without knowing quite what path they'd take to reach the cliff, taking her with him every step.

He raised his head, stared into her heavy eyes. "Shall I test again?" he asked, and without waiting for an answer, released one breast, sliding that hand down her body, slipping his fingers between her thighs again. Her clit felt like a small oiled pearl, and as he rolled it between finger and thumb he imagined dropping to his knees to suck her there. But before he could turn the thought to action, she tensed, gasped and—bang!—she came in a clenching rush, the act of it, the *force* of it, taking Matt completely by surprise.

As she collapsed against him, Matt couldn't think past the ease with which he'd gotten her there. Either she was the most responsive woman he'd ever had or he was a fucking magnificent foreplayer. Whichever, he was euphoric. He loved that her sleepy eyelids were even sleepier, loved the way her breaths were still more like pants, loved the way her nails were digging into his hips. And then she topped it all by nestling her face into his chest and biting him through his T-shirt, and his dick leaped like an animal.

"Two down," he said—no, *snarled*, like a beast. "Two to go."

One more twirl of the fingers that were still between her thighs because he simply couldn't resist. And then he started stripping with a vengeance. Thank God he was barefoot; if he'd had to bend down to take off shoes, he was pretty sure his dick would see it as an opportunity to wrap itself around his neck and strangle him—revenge for making it wait.

His T-shirt was wrenched up and off. Jeans and underwear shoved down, kicked aside. A glance showed a damp patch on his boxer briefs. He'd been leaking pre-cum for so long his poor imprisoned penis had had just about enough. He reached for her, but she stepped back. Prime position to be tumbled on her back on the bed, exactly where he needed her. He reached again.

"No," she said.

Freeze. "No?" It came out disbelievingly.

"Not *that* no," she said. "I mean no as in wait." Her eyes dropped to his dick, which all but lunged at her. He needed a leash for it, that was becoming obvious. "Wait because I want to look at you. First time, you know?"

Jesus God yes, he knew. He took a deep breath to curb the rush in his veins. He could wait while she looked him over. He fucking *loved* that she was looking him over. Another deep breath to calm his body, which had broken out in a sweat.

"Can you make it fast? The looking?" he half asked/ half pleaded. "Because I'd like to move on to some mutual touching."

Her eyes raced over him as he started counting in his head. *One, two, breathe, breathe*, as her eyes snagged on his lower abdominals and she licked her lips. He went taut as a bowstring as he pictured her licking her way up and down the V framing them. *Three—God-help-me—four*. She reached out a finger, touched the top of his dick where more liquid was leaking. *Holy-Mary-mother-of-God—five—six*. She raised her finger to her mouth and sucked it inside.

"Mmm," she said.

And the bowstring twanged, whip-fast, sending his arrow flying. "Fuck this," he said, and launched himself at her.

She landed on her back on the bed, Matt on top of her. A keening moan—hers. A ground-out curse—his. She tried to put her arms around him but he stopped her, forcing them over her head so that her big, beautiful breasts were thrust up at him. He leaned in for one more lick of each nipple, shuddering as her back curved up off the bed, offering him more. His thighs settled between hers, knees splaying to open her, spreading her wide. His hips were pistoning even before his cock was in position. He was so hard he knew he wouldn't need to guide it in. It knew where it had to be and was in a fever to go there. One thrust, and he was inside her, her legs wrapping around him. On his third stroke he felt her heels digging into him, encouraging him to go harder.

He tried to kiss her, but he was too far gone to manage anything except a riotous assault of lips and tongue, goaded on by the fact she was attacking him right back.

He was sweating enough to make sliding off her a real possibility, so he let go of the hands he still had pinioned above her head and wrapped his arms around her, burying his head between her neck and her shoulder, dragging her in so close they were plastered together tightly enough that a tornado wouldn't separate them. Pulse thundering in his ears. Romy almost sobbing as she spurred him on—heels *and* words. "Matt, I'm going to come. Make me, make me, make me come."

And as he felt her internal muscles start to contract around his cock, he unleashed himself, hands moving beneath her bottom, angling her hips, surging into her, aiming for the spot he knew would tip her over.

"Yes, there," she gasped, grinding against him. "God, right *there.*"

Thrust, thrust, fucking thrust, and he felt his own orgasm zap through him. She spasmed around him, crying out his name, and it was as though she'd set a torch to him, so sudden was his eruption, like a gush of lava bursting from a volcano. Gush...then scorching flow. An endless stream, endless pour from him to her. Hot, wet, tight. Delirium.

He stayed, hips bowing into her, as the almost painful tension finally started to drain out of him. He realized he was shivering, but he was still so hot. He had no control over his body, even in the aftermath. Distance. He needed distance. But when he tried to roll off her, she tightened her arms and her legs around him and clung.

"I'm too heavy," he said.

"One minute," she said, her voice muffled because she'd buried her face against his chest. "Just one."

And so Matt stayed on top of her, caught between helplessness and dread at the terrible, aching, never-before closeness. He was relieved when she finally relaxed beneath him, unhooking herself, freeing him.

"I'm fine now," she said, and he eased off her to lie beside her, staring up at the ceiling, not knowing what came next.

She propped herself up on an elbow. "How long do you need to recharge, Matt?"

He angled his head toward her, uncomprehending.

"I'm flying out in the morning, remember, so I need to get back to my hotel soon," she explained. "I need to check my notes for Lennie, and pack, and…and double-check the time of my transfer to the airport. All the things an overthinker does. So if we're going to do it again…" She offered him a tremulous smile. "Well, we're up to petits fours, right?"

Flying out in the morning. Flying. Out. "I thought—" He stopped himself. One night, she'd said. That didn't have to mean *all* night.

But…but he'd thought she'd stay.

Stop! He didn't care if she stayed. It was better if she *didn't* stay.

Safer.

How many goes did it take to get pregnant, anyway? Okay, stupid question. He knew it only took one. It was just a matter of *which* one. A matter of what point in the cycle she was at, and whether the stars were aligning and shit like that.

He thought back to her phone call two weeks ago, when she'd been on day three of her period. If he used that as a guide, they were damn close to target. And when you combined that timing with the fact that he'd shot off inside her like a NASA-grade rocket, she was probably already pregnant. He'd probably given her *trip-*

lets to match the three orgasms. She didn't even have
to stay for her fourth…fourth orgasm…if she didn't…
want…oooohhhh.

Brain slowing down. Blood, heart, nerves, seizing up.
Back up a step. Back up.

She was probably already pregnant. Already…preg-
nant. Already…

Matt reached out a trembling hand, laid it low on
her belly.

Romy stopped breathing, stopped everything, looking
at Matt's hand on her.

She knew what he was thinking, and now that he was
thinking it, she was thinking it, too: she might already
be pregnant.

Way to change the dynamic! A few minutes ago, it
was all about sex. Now it was about more.

She put her hand over his. "So?" she asked softly,
searching his face.

He kept his eyes on their hands. He said nothing but
she felt the shiver that ran through him all the way to
her bone marrow, as though he'd become a part of her.
She wanted to warm him, to rub away the crease between his eyebrows, tell him everything would be okay.

Except that everything wouldn't be okay. His silence
told her that, and the look on his face—a look she'd never
seen on him before. Haunted. Hunted.

They hadn't blurred the line, and they hadn't crossed
it; they'd drawn a new one. And it wasn't a situation
that could be withdrawn from. It was real, and it was
forever. He'd become hers in a way that was different
from before, and she had a sudden insight that he always would be hers, whether she was pregnant or not,

no matter what happened in her life, or who else he slept with. And that was more than he'd bargained on and *way* more than he wanted.

"So," Matt said, and took a deep breath as he eased his hand out from beneath hers. "I'm recharged—let's go for broke this time."

Fast, practiced, blank-faced, he stripped off her socks, and even *that* seemed portentous. Because it felt as though they were no longer erotic—they were just something in his way.

CHAPTER SIX

MATT ENJOYED MORNINGS AFTER. When he was alone, sated, relaxed and a little nostalgic for the previous night's experience even though the details were already hazy.

But this morning, standing in the kitchen Romy hadn't seen even though he'd kitted it out especially for her, he was neither sated nor relaxed. And the details weren't hazy—each one was crystal clear.

Romy, so hesitant going up the stairs.

Romy, diffident and wanting to get it over with once they'd reached the bedroom.

Romy, talking about returning to her hotel room after he'd gone at her like a battering ram.

What did that fucking *tell* him? That she wasn't his speed!

Why hadn't he fucking *listened*? Because he was a fucking monster!

What had he done about it? He'd forged ahead and done her again! Shoving himself into her deep and hard and relentless, wringing a double orgasm out of her, making her beg for it!

And his reward for that brutality was for her to jump out of bed even before she'd stopped gasping his name, grab her clothes as though he'd steal them if she wasn't fast enough, and run for the shower like she couldn't wait to wash him off her skin.

That's when he'd seen the purple marks on her hips, and he'd thanked God she wasn't staying the night after all because he'd have marked her black-and-blue and scraped her raw all over by morning.

He'd pulled on his clothes and waited impatiently for her to reappear from the bathroom, rehearsing apologies, explanations. But when she'd resurfaced, scrubbed and dressed, paper white and jittery, he'd known there was no excuse that would make it right.

"Well, that's that, then," she'd said. And the look on her face as she'd said it had ripped a hole in him. Like she was going to cry, like she was going to *break*.

And so Matt had called her a cab, and trailed after her like a stray dog all the way down that overwrought staircase, and fetched her overcoat and briefcase from the overstuffed library while she waited in the pretentious entrance hall of his mausoleum of a house. And then they'd stood by the door and stared past each other for a million fucking years until the taxi arrived. Then she'd said, "I'll know one way or the other in two weeks, so I'll be in touch then." And with a restrained, chicken-like peck on his cheek, whoosh! She was gone, the door had closed, the taxi was driving away.

Matt had stayed at the door, and it wasn't until three minutes had passed that he'd realized he was waiting for her to come back. Because she *never* left him without hugging him like a maniac and ruffling his hair. He'd actually rested his hand on the door handle, preparing to wrench open the door the moment he heard the cab pull up.

Another minute—no cab.

His knuckles had turned white as it registered that she wasn't coming back. That the peck on the cheek was all he was going to get. That it might be the last thing he ever got from her. And he'd raced up to strip his bed, as though by doing so he could rip the experience out of his room, out of his house, out of his exploding head.

That was when he'd spied the tiny ball of lilac, scrunched up behind the armchair. She'd been so eager to leave, she hadn't even looked for her panties; she'd gone commando—something *his* Romy would never, ever have done because she'd have been all, *What if I get hit by a bus?*

And even knowing that that meant she had to have been in a panic to escape him, he couldn't stop himself from picking up those panties and sniffing them like a sexual deviant, which triggered a leap in his cock that *infuriated* him because those were *Romy's* panties! *His Romy's* panties that he hadn't let himself near for ten fucking years!

He'd grabbed the sheets, screwed them and the panties up together, strode into the bathroom and shoved the lot into the laundry hamper so hard he pushed his hand right through the wickerwork, giving new meaning to the term *basket case*—which he clearly still was the morning after a sleep-deprived night because here he was standing in *her* kitchen, his dick throbbing like the devil, willing her to come back even though he knew she was already in the goddamn air.

"Fuuuuuuuuuuuck!" he yelled, and when that didn't release enough pressure, banged his fist on the counter. "Fuck." Bang. "Fuck." Bang. "*Fuck* this!" And he swept an arm across the kitchen counter, knocking the coffee he'd made for himself but hadn't drunk into the sink.

Fuck the coffee, too! Why was he drinking coffee? He needed an anesthetic, not a stimulant. He wrenched a beer from the fridge—and he was beyond fucking *caring* that Romy always tsk-tsked him out of drinking beer in the morning—and made his way out onto the deck because it was past time for his dick to start behaving like a regular body part and not a Viagra-fueled nightmare and he hoped the frigid wind would knock an inch or two off his erection.

Throwing himself into a seat at his purpose-bought-for-Romy outdoor setting, he took a vicious swig of his beer and forced himself to look out toward San Francisco Bay, where he was going to keep looking until he calmed the fuck down.

An intention that lasted forty seconds, when he experienced an overpowering need to check his cell phone just in case he'd missed a text message from Romy.

Aaaand nope. Moron. If he hadn't gotten a text by now he wasn't going to get one, because she was *already-in-the-goddamn-air*-how-long-did-it-take-to-get-that-through-his-head!

He tossed his phone onto the table, only to pick it up again immediately to call up the message Romy had sent him after their phone call two weeks ago—the selfie, in which she was blowing him a kiss. "My hero" was the text that accompanied it. He'd rolled his eyes at that, but he'd laughed, too, because her mouth was too wide for that expression to be anything other than comical. Maybe seeing it now would give him hope that the two of them might laugh about last night in due course.

But when he pulled up the photo, instead of laughing at her duckbill lips, he found himself running his fingertip over them while his breathing went haywire and his heartbeat went bump-bump-thump and he could almost…taste her.

He snatched his hand away from the phone, picked up his beer, took another swig. But swilling the beer around his mouth did nothing to disperse the taste of her, which seemed to have drenched him at some cellular level.

She should be here, telling him he was still her hero even though he knew he was an asshole. She should be here, forgiving him the way she said she always would. She should be here, easing his rage the way being around her always did—that bitter strangle of fury he'd been carrying inside forever, forever, for ever, at what his parents had turned him into. This…*thing*, dark and twisted and disgusting, that made him not good enough for her.

"Fuuuuuuuuuuuck!" Another gut-wrenching yell. Because he wanted her here…and yet he should be glad she wasn't. He'd spent ten careful years keeping her away, blocking every sexual thought of her, trying not to ruin what he'd felt that first night he'd met her, that glimmering sense of comfort she gave him.

It was ever-after stuff, what he'd felt that night. And what he'd felt for her had stayed in the realm of ever-after through three and a half years' living in the same house, through six and a half years' living on different continents, through the past two weeks of knowing the baby was his gateway to a permanent link with her because she'd have only one child and that child would be his and whoever came after him could therefore *never* take his place in her life.

If he were a decent human being, he would have told her everything about himself and given her the chance to find better sperm. But he could live with not being a decent human being. He'd lived with it a hell of a long time now.

He reached for his beer, saw that his hand was shaking and took a long, painful breath.

If he'd succeeded in accomplishing the ultimate betrayal and impregnating her, would she hate the thought of having his child, after last night? And if she *wasn't* pregnant, would she write him off and look elsewhere?

Two weeks, and he'd know. Two weeks—that's when she'd said she'd be in touch.

Although he could contact her, couldn't he? He could text her now, if he wanted to.

He picked up his phone again, racking his brain for something funny to say. Maybe something about preparing the kid for a lifetime of dealing with redhead jokes…?

But…no. She might get all serious and tell him again that she loved his red hair. Loved his hair…loved everything about him…loved…him…?

No!

No, she couldn't tell him that. He wouldn't let her tell him that.

The text would have to be something simple like checking she got home all right. He always sent that text when she was flying home. And it never mattered that he sent it while she was in the air, because she got it when she landed and she always responded straightaway and that way it would be only hours—not two weeks— before he heard from her.

He tapped out the message…and then froze.

What the fuck was he doing?

She'd said two weeks. The inference being she didn't *want* to be in touch until then.

Was he going to start hounding her when she didn't want to be hounded? After he'd *told* her he didn't do that stalking shit? Why make her more uncomfortable with him than she already was?

Nope. Delete. Delete that message. Delete, delete, DELETE, GODDAMMIT!

He realized he was about to crack the case on his cell phone, and forced himself to ease his grip. He threw the phone down, got up and strode over to the edge of the deck. The view was the only thing he liked about this house. He should be out on that damn bay, kayaking. It would be worth freezing his ass off to get out of the house.

He strode back to the table, scooped up his phone—in case a message came through—shoved it in his pocket—because he knew it wouldn't—and headed inside to the library to find his kayaking map because no way was he taking his cell phone with him; odds were instead of using it to check his coordinates he'd obsess about text messages he wasn't getting and didn't want to *think* about getting.

But once in the library he was drawn to the desk, where Romy's paperwork was, and he lost interest in looking for the map. He could see her, even with his eyes open, muttering to herself as she flicked through pages. And when he closed his eyes… Oh God, the images. Furtive flashes of naked bodies, eager thrusts, cries and tongues and fevered flesh.

His eyes bolted open. "Jesus Christ, stop!" he cried.

And as if in answer to a prayer, his cell phone pinged with an incoming text.

Bump-bump-thump went his heart.

Romy!

So she hadn't caught her flight. She was still in San Francisco.

He put his hand over the phone in his pocket and smiled. She'd forgiven him.

Call or text back?

Call, he decided. He'd suggest she come over and hang out here, strictly friend zone now their one-night stand was over. He'd remind her about the paella she owed him and then help her make it, and they could eat it while watching a movie—there was a TV behind a panel in this godforsaken library and it didn't get more innocent than watching a movie; they always watched movies together when she was over. He fumbled the phone out. He'd get her new flight details, drive her to the airport at the appointed time the way he usually did, when she wasn't running for her life. And if she didn't hug him goodbye he'd headlock her!

He swiped his cell on. It would all be back to norm—

"Shit." As he saw who the message was from.

Not Romy, Camilla.

Coffee? Can meet you in ten.

Coffee. Camilla's daytime euphemism for sex. Nighttime was margarita.

Well, obviously *that* wasn't going to happen. A guy who'd offered to impregnate a friend didn't fuck his way around town until the job was done. Still…hmm…any red-blooded man would get a libidinous spark at the thought of sex with Camilla—so why wasn't he?

He tried picturing Camilla. Honey-blond hair; aquamarine eyes; sharp, high cheekbones; pouty mouth; curved in all the right places and perfectly proportioned. A very beautiful woman. She was fun, too. She laughed a lot; she ate like a normal person and drank beer. She was even clued up on tech talk, unlike Romy, who thought the only Java that existed was an island in Indonesia. He *liked* Camilla. They were good together. They thought alike. And she was the type to flay the flesh off a guy—literally, not metaphorically—which was exactly what he needed at that moment, a physical pain to replace the other kind.

He tried to coax some hot blood into his veins, some rigidity into his cock. But it was no use. His veins remained disinterested. His penis positively *un*interested—in fact, it was...deflating...? Oh God, he really was deflating!

He sighed, and sent back a simple text to Camilla of the sorry-no-can-do-some-other-time variety. Then he stared at the phone some more, but no matter how long he stared, no text from Romy materialized.

He shoved the phone into his pocket. He was going to go back to his bedroom. He was going to take the sheets out of the hamper and rip the fuckers in half.

He was three strides to the door when he recalled that there was a pair of lilac panties in with the sheets and—whooshka—up came his dick, like an amphetamine-loaded cobra from a snake charmer's basket. Un-fucking-*bearable*.

He whirled again, returned to the windows, desperate to calm down, but there was no calm to be had out there. Swollen gray clouds were gathering over the bay, like they were building apace with his turbulent mood. The weather wouldn't stop him taking out the kayak—in fact, he relished the idea of carving through the water in a storm.

He watched until the first raindrops dotted the win-

dow…gathered power…started pelting. He turned into
the room, strode to the desk, looked down at those
motherfucking pages. Their only saving grace was
that Teague hadn't drawn them up; he'd hate to have
to beat the crap out of Teague for getting between him
and Romy.

Not that the documents really mattered. The crux of
the deal was that Matt's name wouldn't be on the birth
certificate. He didn't need fifteen documents to confirm
he wasn't going to be a real father.

He picked up a three-page document at random and
ripped it in half. An action that reminded him of what he
wanted to do to his sheets, so he ripped it again. Again.
Again. He hated those fucking pages. Rip, rip, fucking
rip. To the next document. Rip. Rip. Over and over and
over, page after page.

He was breathing heavily by the time he'd finished
his harried tearing and looked at the pieces scattered
across the desktop. What a mess. An all-round fucking
mess. On the desk, and in his head.

It wasn't meant to be like this. It was meant to be
easy. A carefree donation of easily produced body fluid.
So why had it felt like something else, something more,
last night?

Oh God, why could he *see* her so clearly? His red-
haired, hazel-eyed daughter, looking at him with the
same quiet trust he'd seen in Romy's eyes last night.

He didn't know how to banish that image; he didn't
know how to fix him and Romy; he didn't know how to
stop wanting forever; he didn't know how to reconcile
all those things into a way of existing that didn't feel
like he was being ripped into pieces, like those fucking
pages on the desk.

He rubbed his fingertips up and down his forehead, trying to ease the ache that was building in his head. His sinuses felt swollen. The back of his nose was stinging. He blinked hard and swallowed against a sudden lump in his throat. Swallowed again, but the lump remained.

He imagined getting Romy's regular parcel of photos, and that in with the shots of her parents, a guy she might be dating, restaurant dishes she was about to consume and shoes she needed a second opinion on before purchase, were photos of his daughter. The birth. The home-from-the-hospital shot. First tooth. First crawl. First birthday. First walk. First day at school. First French fucking snail being eaten. Photos of a normal kid, who had a normal mother and normal grandparents. A normal, innocent childhood.

He spun away from the desk, strode to the window, kicked aside the ruined curtains, stared out. The rain was pelting down now. "If only..." he said, conscious of a horrible, clawing, push-pull need in his life for less... and yet more. He placed the palms of his hands on the glass, wishing he could feel the storm. "If only..." But he blocked the thought before he could finish it. No point in going there.

The back of his nose was stinging again, and there was a crushing ache in his chest.

There was no use pretending he didn't know what it was.

It was grief.

And it was out of his control.

CHAPTER SEVEN

NOT PREGNANT.

Not.

A month had passed since San Francisco, and Romy, sitting at her computer with her email account open, knew she could no longer put off telling Matt.

She should have done it the instant she'd gotten her period two weeks ago, but she'd had a minimeltdown in the bathroom and bawled her eyes out instead.

And then the cramps had hit, the pain going all-out to completely incapacitate her as though punishing her for daring to do what she'd done with Matt—and surely agony was a valid excuse for delaying the call.

Disbelief had come next. With all Matt's potency, delivered at the right time of the month, it was *inconceivable* that she wasn't pregnant. So maybe her uterus was playing a last, loathsome trick on her and she *wasn't* not-pregnant after all.

That had bought her a week.

But today, when Lennie had called to ask her to return to San Francisco because he'd finally made a decision and needed her to scout out a definite location for his restaurant, it was a case of time's up. Within two minutes of peeing on the stick of her home pregnancy kit, she'd burst into tears again.

And now, sitting at her computer, she knew there'd only ever been one honest reason for not telling Matt two weeks ago: fear that the instant he knew, she'd lose him.

Okay, that wasn't quite true. It was more that the instant he knew, she'd have to accept that she'd *already* lost him. She could even pinpoint the exact moment it had happened: when he'd put his hand where their baby might have been and what he'd done had become real.

The mind-blowing sex he'd almost immediately launched into made no sense after that…but Romy had a nagging feeling that if she figured out what had motivated him to "go for broke" following that club to the head, she'd have the key to the tower Matt kept himself barricaded in.

Not that she'd had time to test any locks! The vortex into which he'd hurled her had been so wild, she hadn't been able to so much as catch her breath from start to finish. No words, no instruction, no invitation—just his touch driving her inexorably on until her eyes rolled back in her head and her toes curled. The crescendo? Two soaring, thrilling orgasms, the last one adroitly, effortlessly, synchronized to his own.

And yet despite his almost slavish attention to her pleasure, and despite that careful synchronization she though may well have curled his toes, too, she'd felt… alone. Flung away, like an electric guitar that had been played for maximum flash and drama before being pounded onto the stage and obliterated.

Her self-preservation instincts had kicked in, and she was up, preparing to leave, desperate not to face being Matt's first-ever regret.

She'd reached for her mobile phone so many times that night, wanting to jump back over that crossed line and at least open the door to reclaiming their friendship, but every time she'd started a text, she'd lost her nerve. There'd been no adequate words for what she was feeling. Or at least, none he'd want to hear. Don't call it love, he'd said, and she hadn't, she wouldn't. But she had no other words, either.

So here she was, still with no words, effectively in limbo, with Matt's email address staring accusingly at her from the To box above the blank message space.

She scrubbed her hands over her face. Had it really been only six weeks since that phone call, when Matt had assured her having a baby would be the easiest thing in the world?

She closed her eyes, steeling herself to call up the image of his face after he'd come inside her that first time—the bleakness of it. To remember the way his expression had changed to something cool and calculating as he'd said, *I'm recharged—let's go for broke this time.* The silence as he'd walked her downstairs. The desolation in his eyes when she'd kissed his cheek—as though in going for broke, he'd broken *himself.*

And she knew what she had to do was formally, officially, let him go.

She opened her eyes, and started typing.

Hi, Matt
The big news is I'm not pregnant, so no Yippie-Kai-Yay motherfucker just yet.

Been thinking that with you there and me here and all that paperwork we never got to the end of, a donor closer to home makes more sense. So consider this an official notification that Plan A is extinct—in other words you're off the hook, services no longer required.

She paused there, not sure how to sign off.

Would these be her last words to Matt? If so, she knew what she'd want them to be. She'd broken the cardinal rule before she'd known it existed and said them in her heart ten years ago. She may not have said the words aloud but she wanted to. She was *tired* of keeping them inside. So tired, her fingers trembled on the keyboard with the need to type them…

I love you

Almost by magic the words were there on the screen. Her heart raced as she read them; she knew if she sent them it really would be over.

In which case, wouldn't the words be useless?

If she wanted to get him back into her life she had to be more strategic. She had to let him know there was a cleared path back to their old friendship…but only if he chose to tread it. And so she deleted those three words and tapped out a new closer. Light and bright and cool and unthreatening:

But I owe you a favor of your choice for giving it the old college try. If you're still hankering for paella, I've got a new twist on the old recipe so give me a shout when you're next in London if you'd like to collect.
Romy
X

And then she hit Send, closed her laptop and burst into tears.

CHAPTER EIGHT

"I NEVER PRETENDED to be a computer whiz," Romy said, bringing Teague's fourth cup of coffee over to him.

"Neither did I," Teague said, "so say a prayer that between us we haven't lost everything while you *open that damn door*! With any luck it'll be Matt, come to save us."

She checked, but only for an instant, at hearing Matt's name. "It won't be him." She plonked Teague's coffee on the dining table beside her laptop, within reach of his hand. "So keep going. And remember, you can lose anything you like as long as you find the—"

"Romy—the door—I beg you."

"—Lennie_SanFrancisco file," she finished, before heading for the door, calling out an en route "Keep your shirt on!" to whoever was outside.

She swung the door open…and her mouth snap-froze in a gape.

Her heart jolted, then hammered, as Matt—it really, astoundingly, unbelievably, *was* Matt!—lowered the clenched fist he'd raised as though preparing to pound a hole through the wood.

When had she sent her email? She counted back, lightning fast. Less than twenty-four hours ago. If her email was responsible for rocketing Matt across the Atlantic, was that a positive, negative or neutral development? She didn't know, couldn't work it out because her thoughts were flying past each other, refusing to land.

"Keep my shirt on?" Matt asked, sounding oddly breathless, and when one corner of his mouth quirked up in a rueful smile, her thoughts stopped flying and stuttered to a halt. "You sure about that?"

Shirt. On. Here. London. Matt! Gorgeous.

Her brain was too mangled to form actual sentences and her mouth was too dry to say them. She was reduced to stepping back and vaguely beckoning with her hand, a mute version of *Come in*.

Matt stepped over the threshold, and ever-careless of his possessions, ignored the coat stand to drop his overcoat on the floor along with his duffel bag. For a hopeful moment, Romy thought he was going to pull her into his arms, but a sound behind her—Teague's chair scraping against the floor—distracted him.

"Yay! The hero arrives!" Teague said.

Shock sparked in Matt's eyes as he looked past her, but when Romy turned to uncover the problem all she found was Teague looking at them over the top of her laptop screen.

"Uh-oh," Teague said.

Uh-oh? Romy's eyes went from Teague to a now-expressionless Matt.

"Just to be clear, Matt," Teague said, "all I was doing was reinstalling Windows for her."

"I'll finish it," Matt said.

"It's finished. But by all means check what I did."

Romy looked from Matt to Teague this time. Something was wrong.

Teague closed her laptop and made his way over to them.

"But…are you leaving?" she asked him as he retrieved his overcoat from the stand.

"Yes, Romy, I am."

"Where are you going?"

Shrugging into his coat. "Back to my hotel."

"Why?"

Grabbing his scarf. "Because dinner appears to be canceled."

"It's *not* canceled!" Romy said, and turned to Matt. "Tell him to stay." Getting nothing from that quarter, she tennis-balled back to Teague. "Teague!"

Teague laugh-winced. "Are you trying to get me killed, Romes?"

"What? No! I mean— What?"

Teague's response was to look squarely at Matt as he draped his scarf around his neck. "Just one thing," he said. "Prove to her I've recovered the Lennie_SanFrancisco file or you'll have a meltdown on your hands. She's got a meeting with him tomorrow."

"Fuck Lennie!" Matt said with extreme loathing.

Teague grinned. "He *wishes* she would, anyway!" He knotted his scarf. "But it's your job to rescue her if Lennie steps out of line, isn't it?"

Matt's eyes narrowed. "What's that supposed to mean?"

"It means you'll swoop in to save Romy's day, as usual."

In the hanging moment that followed, Romy found herself holding her breath. She could feel tension rolling off Matt in thick waves, but his voice was calm when she asked, "Do *you* want the job, Teague?" Almost *too* calm.

"Oh, I can't do *that* job," Teague said. "Lennie's not scared of me."

"What makes you think he's scared of *me*?"

Teague kept his gaze steady on Matt. "Intuition."

Matt made an infinitesimal adjustment to his stance. "Are *you* scared of me, Teague?"

"No," Teague said. "Because *I* know *you* know I'm not a threat."

On the verge of passing out from oxygen deprivation, Romy took in a tiny breath, then held it again when Matt made a sound like a cut-off growl as Teague pulled her into his arms for a hug.

"Call me if you need me, Romes, okay?" Teague said in a stage whisper, before letting her go. "But now, if you'll excuse me…"

"Wait!" Romy cried, and caught Teague's hand. "You don't have to leave!"

Teague squeezed then released her fingers. "Yes, Romy, I do."

"Then…then at least let me walk with you to the train station and…and explain," she urged—even though she didn't know what the explanation *was*.

Teague touched her cheek briefly. "I don't need an explanation. And I'd prefer it if you stayed to soothe the savage beast." He flashed her a whiter-than-snow smile. "For *all* our sakes, hmm?"

And then he clapped a hand briefly on Matt's shoulder, said, "Play nice with my girl," and left.

Romy stared at the door after it clicked shut behind Teague, trying to figure out what had just happened.

She sensed Matt moving, heard him settling into Teague's chair at the dining table. *Play nice with my girl*, Teague had adjured him. But Matt didn't appear to be in a "nice" mood.

Or maybe…thinking back to Matt's smile as she'd

opened the door…maybe seeing Teague had *changed* Matt's mood. It had certainly upped the testosterone quotient. But that would mean Matt was jealous, wouldn't it? And he was *never* jealous. He didn't *care* enough to be jealous. Or maybe…maybe he did…?

She turned, intrigued by that notion, to find Matt tapping away at her computer, and cleared her throat to get his attention.

Matt ignored her. And that was interesting, because he'd never ignored her before and she was *p-r-e-t-t-y* sure he hadn't flown all the way from San Francisco just to do so now.

So why *was* he here? Question of the day.

She took two steps, and cleared her throat again. "Are you going to tell me why you're here, Matt?"

He stilled, eyes on her keyboard. "Are you going to tell me why *Teague* was here?" And then he raised his eyes, pinning her in place. "Because fixing your computer is *my* job, isn't it?"

Okay, that definitely smacked of *some* kind of jealousy, and it made her heart flutter like a leaf in a storm. "You were in San Francisco."

"I've installed updates on your computer remotely before."

"It's just…he was here."

"So I noticed."

"For dinner."

"So I gathered."

"He's working on a big corporate merger, and one of the parties is British so he's here for a couple of weeks and he called me and I offered to cook—just like I do for *you* when you're here. And when he arrived, I mentioned my computer problems, and…" She stopped, threw up

her hands. "Why am I explaining this? I've done nothing wrong."

"Why *are* you explaining, if you've done nothing
wrong?"

"Probably because you're glaring at me, making me
think I've done something wrong. He came—he saw—
he fixed. The end. Unless you want to know the dinner menu, in which case it was supposed to be steak
and ale pie."

Matt leaned back in his chair. "Let me ask a different question. When did he arrive in London? Could it
possibly have been *yesterday*?"

"Yes, so what?"

"So that gives me some context for that 'closer to
home' reference in your email."

"You mean…? No, you *can't* mean—! *Teague?*
Teague lives in *Manhattan*. How's that close to London?"

"He's here now. Ergo, close."

"As are you—so *what*?"

"So it finally makes sense why you took so long to
contact me."

"You mean…?" But she shook her head. "*What* do
you mean?"

"I mean I hear nothing from you for a month, but then
Teague arrives and—wham!—notice to terminate my
services comes flying through cyberspace."

She stared at him while that sifted through her foggy
brain. And then, "Oh. My God!" she said. "You cannot
be serious."

"And yet I am."

She came storming over to the table as four weeks of
pent-up emotion ruptured. "You *dare* to tick me off for
not contacting you? You didn't send me one text! One

email! I didn't get a phone call, a Facebook message, nothing! I had to fill the void by overthinking every damn thing that had happened in San Francisco until I thought I'd go crazy!"

"I've been hanging on the edge of my fucking seat waiting for two fucking words from you—not pregnant. A few seconds is all it would have taken!"

"Oh! Oh! You were *not* hanging on the edge of your seat! You made it crystal clear you'd lost interest in the whole thing even before I left your house! I saw your face, Matt, when it hit you—it hit you like a ton of bricks—what you'd let yourself in for, that maybe, just maybe, that boring paperwork I wanted to go through with you was worth reading after all!"

"I tore up that paperwork!"

"You—you—"

"*Bastard* is the word I think we agreed on in San Francisco."

"You bastard!" she rapped out.

He set his jaw. "Which doesn't change the fact that *you* were supposed to contact *me*, goddammit!"

"And I *did*!"

He banged his hand on the table. "Two weeks *late*!"

"Well, excuse me for not being buoyed with optimism by your last words to me. 'Let's go for broke this time'! It took me the whole month to get over that!"

He pushed his chair back from the table, jumped to his feet. "I told you to stop me if you didn't like what I did!"

"It wasn't that *I* didn't like it, it was that *you* didn't. That last time was a performance—a bravura performance but definitely a performance, even if you didn't really want to give it."

"That wasn't a performance, Romy, that was me. What I *am*. What I *like*."

"You didn't like *anything* after you realized I might be pregnant. You couldn't even muster up a goodbye when I left!"

"You didn't give me *time* to say goodbye. You ran out on me like your ass was on fire."

"You could have stopped me!"

"I don't stop women from leaving me, remember? You want to leave, you leave!"

"If you believe that, why are you here?"

Split second while he stared at her. And then, "Good question!" he snarled, and strode for the door.

She hurried after him. "What are you doing?"

"Figure it out," he said, and reefed his overcoat up off the floor, one-handed.

"Matt!"

Up came his bag. Flung over his shoulder.

She grabbed his arm. "You're not leaving until we talk this through."

He jerked away from her. "Read your own fucking email. You talked it through for both of us."

"What is the problem? If you want to try again, we'll just…try again!"

"No, Romy, we won't. It's too dangerous. *I'm* too dangerous." And he turned to the door again.

"No!" she cried, and dragged his overcoat from him, threw it back on the floor. "What are you talking about?"

"I saw the bruises, okay?"

"They were nothing!" Romy cried.

He reached for his coat again—she blocked him. "If that's really what's bothering you—a few love bites— I'll put some on you right now and we'll be even."

"That's not funny."

"No, it's not funny, if you think I'm some delicate flower who can't handle some enthusiastic sex! So read my lips: You. Didn't. Hurt me. You didn't. And you're not going to leave me like this after keeping me hanging for a month."

"You left *me*, Romy," he said to her.

"Only because you *wanted* me to go."

"Bullshit. I asked you to stay the night."

"That was *before*."

"Before *what*? Before you moved the goalposts? Before you replaced ten years with one night on a fucking *whim*? Plan B! Jesus! What made you think that was going to work with someone like me?"

"Someone like you? What does that even mean?"

"It means your email hit the nail on the head—I'm *not* the man for the job. I don't *want* the job. So…so sign Teague up! I don't care."

"What *is* it about Teague tonight? It's just Teague—same old Teague! But it's like you're suddenly jealous of him!"

He recoiled. "I'm not jealous of Teague."

"Then what was all that about when you arrived?"

"Not jealousy. Not…what you think."

She rolled her eyes. "Okay."

"I mean it!"

"Okay!"

"I *mean* it, Romy! I'm the opposite of jealous! I *want* him to have you. I *always* wanted him to have you. That's why I introduced him to you in the first place. He's a fucking saint! There's no one better for you."

She blinked at him—once, twice, slowly—and she finally understood why Matt called it the blink of insanity when she did that: because she was blinking at a stark, staring madman. "Oh my God," she said. "You want him to *have* me? What am I? A reward for good behavior?"

"You've got it ass-end around, Romy, I want *you* to have *him*."

"And what about what I want for myself?"

"We're *talking* about what you want—a clean-cut, solid-gold hero."

"No, Matt. If we were talking about what I want, we'd be talking about you."

"Romy, you only *think*—"

"*Don't* tell me what I think! If I wanted to have sex with Teague I'd have done it when we were dating!"

"But this is about more than sex. It's about sharing a baby, raising a baby, providing the best for a baby."

"And if I'd wanted to have a *baby* with Teague, I'd have turned down your offer and called him straight up to ask him!"

"So ask him! Go on! You know it'll be better with him."

"And if I asked him, what do you think he'd say?"

"He'd say yes." He tore his hands through his hair. "Ah Jesus, he'd say yes."

"He'd say *Let's wait, Romy*, that's what he'd say. He'd say *Let's think it through. Let's do the* math. *Let's get the fucking* paperwork *in order. And meanwhile, Romy, why don't you get your own lawyer to look into precedents, even though I'm a lawyer myself, because two lawyers are better than one, and maybe go back to the doctor for some stronger painkillers and bleed your goddamn life out while I think it through, and then when you're sure you're sure and I'm* sure, *we'll get married and then we'll start trying.*"

"And that's what you wanted—due process."

"No! No! I don't want another version of myself! I want what *you* did! What *you* offered is what I want. Fast and brave and unthinking and…and fuck-it-all, let's just do it. That's what I want. And you! I wanted *you*! I want you still."

"Stop, Romy!"

"No, I won't stop. You turn up here, all but scare Teague out of the flat for what reason I have *no fucking idea* since you're *not fucking jealous*, and then you tell me I'm supposed to fall into Teague's arms because you think that'll work better for me? Well, the answer is no! I'm not doing it. I remember very well that you got me and Teague together in college. I also remember you never asked why we split up."

"Because it didn't matter why."

"Of course it mattered! But I think you *knew* why we split up. And I think you didn't want to face it. Well, I want you to face it. So in case you *don't* know, I'm going to tell you—it's because I couldn't love him. And the reason I couldn't love him is because I already loved—"

"No!" he said, cutting her off.

"Why *not*?"

"Because it'll be the end. Don't. Say it. Don't, Romy."

"Not saying it out loud won't change the truth."

He grabbed her right hand, lifted it. "Wanna know about love? It's *this*. He gave you his dead sister's ring even though you'd been broken up for two and a half years. What does that tell you?"

"That he knew I'd cherish it."

"The way he cherishes *you*."

"No!" she said.

"Not saying it out loud won't change the truth," he

said, throwing her own words back at her. "You want love—he'll give it to you. I won't."

"We're friends. Teague and I are *friends*."

"What do you think you and I are?"

"I don't... I want... I don't know anymore."

"Having sex didn't make us more than friends, Romy—all it made us is friends with *benefits*. Benefits that were supposed to accrue to *you*. And who knows? If you'd stayed the night those benefits may have had more of a chance to accrue. Well, spilt milk, water under the bridge, whatever—you cut things short. So stand by that decision, because your instinct was right—I'm not the best man for this. And if the friend dynamic is what's bothering you about Teague, let me tell you that I've had sex with friends before and I will again. So I suggest you accept that you *can* have sex with friends, take another look at Teague and the next time he gives you a ring it'll have a whopping big diamond in it."

"I don't want a diamond."

"Yeah, well, even without the diamond, compare his platinum ring to what I gave you for your twenty-first birthday. A computer game. I mean, seriously! There's the difference between him and me right there on your finger."

"You gave me *shares*, Matt, not a computer game. Shares in Artie's start-up gaming company. Shares he wanted to be *yours*, not mine."

"They were worthless."

"And now they're not."

"Yeah, well, as I've said before, money's an easy thing for me to give."

"Those shares weren't money to you. They came from that soul you say you don't have."

He flung her hand away. "Oh, for fuck's sake! Don't worry about my soul, Romy—protect your own. Or I may yet give in to my baser urgings and steal it."

"Oh, Matt, can't you see? You don't *have* to steal my soul. I'll give it to you willingly. I'll *gift wrap* it for you. I'll change it to suit you, twist into any shape you want, paint it any color you like."

He grabbed her by the upper arms and pulled her in close, looking down at her with such an intense mix of fury and fuck me, a sliver of almost-pleasurable fear shimmied down her spine. "Make it pitch-black and we might have a deal," he said.

"I said any color—I meant it."

"I've told you before, Romy, be careful what you say. What you open the door to. There are wolves out there—wolves like me."

"Then teach me to be a wolf."

"A kitten can't become a wolf."

"What can I do to convince you?"

"Nothing."

"What about if I…if I bite you?"

He laughed.

"I mean it. It's what I've always wanted to do. Bite a man through the skin until I draw blood. There. That's my deepest, darkest fantasy. What do you think about that?"

He released her, stepped back, tilted his head to one side and dragged at his sweater, the T-shirt beneath, to expose his neck to her. "Go ahead, Vampira."

She swallowed. "I…"

He laughed again. Released his sweater. "You're *not. My. Speed.*"

Her eyes flickered downward, to the front of his jeans. "I don't believe you."

"As you said—that's always there."

"As you said—you wouldn't be able to function like a human if it was."

"I'm not much of a human. And my services are no longer required, remember?"

"And yet, knowing that…here you are."

"I came because we had unfinished business."

"Then finish it!"

"It was finished the minute I walked in the door and saw him."

"Prove it's finished. Kiss me."

"No."

"Then don't kiss me. Fuck me."

CHAPTER NINE

"ASKING TO BE fucked isn't enough to bring you down to my level," he said, but although his voice carried the right amount of sneer, desire raced through him so fast he trembled with it.

She straightened her spine, and it made his heart lurch. God, she'd always been a straight arrow. The straightest. "Then tell me what will," she said.

He retook her right hand, brought it to his mouth, licked the problematic platinum band, then sucked her pinky finger into his mouth. He watched her as he sucked, as he kept sucking. *Stop me, stop me, Romy*, he pleaded silently, because he hated himself for what he was about to ask.

But she didn't stop him. She did nothing except close her eyes, and then open them as though she wouldn't allow herself that weakness. He slipped his mouth from her finger, slowly, insolently, but kept hold of her hand. "Taking off his ring will be a start. Do that and I'll fuck you."

He saw her eyes go wide, the swallow she took. But she tipped up her chin and threw his challenge back at him. "I won't make what's between us about Teague. It has *nothing* to do with him."

"It has everything to do with him. I'm the bit of rough you have on the side—he's the one you go home to. You don't take off the ring of the man you go home to."

"I came home to *you*, Matt. For three and a half years I came home to you. After every man, I came home to you. And you...you came home to me."

"Oh, Romy." He had to touch her. Had to. Just once. So he cupped her cheek, even though he knew she'd feel the fine quivering in his fingers. "I could count your men on one hand. And there's the difference. Do you have any idea how many sex partners I've had?"

She brought her hand up to cover his, keeping it there. "I only care that it took ten years to make me one of them."

"But you were only one of them for a night," he said. "And you won't be again unless you take off his ring."

"If it's so important to you, *you* take it off. Take it to Teague. Tell him everything. Tell him the reason I always wear it is because I feel guilty for not...not loving him the way you seem to think I should. But do it *after*, not before, so I know this is about me, not him."

"And if I insist on doing it now?"

"You won't. I know you won't. You stopped me so many times in San Francisco, making sure I was okay, making sure I hadn't changed my mind. You said you wouldn't do anything I didn't like—and you didn't. I know you won't do anything I don't want you to do now, either. You're not the man you're trying so hard to tell me you are."

And that was when he lost it, as though he could hear a snap in his brain, and he crushed her against his chest. How could he want to be her hero and yet simultaneously need to show her that he'd be her downfall? He was confused, and crazy with lust for her, and so damn tired of not having her.

"So be my type all the way now. *Mine*, not his," he said, and ground his cock against her to let her know exactly what his type was.

And *God*, she felt good. Plump and fragrant and perfect. A delicious tremble ran through her and he loved the feel of it so much he ground his cock against her again.

"Do you like that?" he asked.

"Yes," she gasped.

"My cock?"

"Yes."

"You can't even say the word, can you?"

"Cock. Your cock."

"And if I said I wanted to see you on your knees for me, with my cock in your mouth, sucking?"

"I'd do it."

"Say it, Romy."

"I want to suck your cock."

"Would you do anything I ask?"

"Anything!" she moaned, her hips arching helplessly into him as he rubbed himself against her again. "Oh God, it isn't fair to torment me like this."

His mouth hovered over hers. "You want fair? Then hear me. I don't care about your heart, or your soul. I care about your body, for a limited time only. And all that's of interest to me right now is if…" grind "you're…" grind "wet!"

A whimper reached past the whoosh of his pulse in his ears, but no words. He wished he could see her eyes, but they were tightly closed now. It was hard to see her so lost in passion, knowing he wanted to be more for her, to be better for her, and yet be unable to convince himself that was possible. But he was helpless. He would take her, lost or found, his or Teague's or anyone else's, any way at all, even though he didn't deserve her, and pray that this time he'd get her out of his burning blood so he could leave her alone.

He ground himself against her again, more urgently now, and she edged her thighs slightly apart. "Tell me, Romy. Hurry. Tell me you're ready, you're wet and ready enough for me."

Her eyes bolted open. "I'm not telling you—you'll have to find out for yours—"

It was as far as she got, because Matt found he couldn't wait another second to put his mouth on hers. Not gently. He couldn't be gentle. He wanted her too much. No more words. No taunts. No dares. No time. He needed her on his tongue, needed her limbs and her breaths tangled with his. He needed to be closer, sur-rounding her, inside her.

For the longest moment she stayed with him, and then she moaned against his mouth and it seemed to snap her back to reality. She bolted against him and struggled free, and then stared up at him, her breaths coming in sharp bursts, her magnificent chest heaving.

Had he scared her off already? "Romy," he said. Just her name, but there was a plea in it—a plea both to stop him and to not stop him.

She gave a cry of surrender, flung herself into his arms again, kissed him so hard their teeth crashed to-gether and he fucking exulted in it. It wasn't anything soft that she was offering, nothing comfortable. No more stopping. No backing out. So when she eased slightly away, a murmur of apology for hurting him on her lips,

he used his hand on the back of her head to jam her
mouth against his and instantly she gave herself up to
him. A drench of heat, back and forth between them.
He shoved one thigh roughly between her legs, and she
surged against him. A drugging, sucking kiss. A wan-
ton, blazing kiss.

When he broke to breathe, he kept his mouth close
enough to taste her. "Tell me it's me you want, that I'm
the only one."

"Yes!" she said, surging against him. "You, I want
you, any way you want to be."

"Only me."

"Only you." She shoved his chest. "There." Another
shove. "Satisfied? Now do it!"

God, the triumph of it! He didn't care if she shoved
him through the nearest wall as long as she meant those
words. It was wrong to want to hear them, worse to *ask*
to hear them, but he needed them. A kind of forgiveness, permission to be exactly who he was, to be only
what he could.

"Am I satisfied?" he asked, and framing her face with
his hands, he kissed her harder still. "I won't be satisfied until I'm buried inside you."

Another rough kiss, hot and wet. Her hands were at
the front of his jeans, unbuttoning, unzipping him, and
he wondered how long he'd last when he'd been starving
for her for so long. Mouths crushing, bruising, a clash
of teeth and tongue, his heartbeat going crazy, excitement fizzing in his blood.

He kept kissing her, couldn't seem to stop, as he
dragged her jeans halfway down her legs. Unable to
wait another inch, he ripped off her panties. He wanted
to tear every stitch of her clothing and rend from her life

everything that had kept her from him for four unfathomable weeks, for ten clueless years.

Romy's hands were under his sweater, under his T-shirt, skating up his chest. He wished she'd rake him with her nails and make him bleed for her. And as if answering that need in him, she dug her fingernails in. He drew back, not to stop her but to see her as she marked him, and the ferociousness in her face made him kiss her again. Wanting him made her angry. Well, he was with her there, furious at how much he wanted this with her. So if a bit of fierce would bring them to terms with what was between them, then he'd *give* her fierce.

He untethered the last of his restraint, hauling her to the floor and under him, his cock lunging even though her legs weren't open to him. He was going to take her here, now. He was going to pretend there was no choice, even though he knew the choice would be waiting at the end of whatever they did.

Her jeans were manacling her legs, but he couldn't bear to let her go long enough to release her from the bind. His cock wasn't going to wait; it was weeping for her already. He'd have to take her as she was, even though she'd be so tight in that position he'd likely explode the moment he was inside her. He tore his mouth free and dragged in a tortured breath.

"Hurry, hurry," she pleaded, struggling against the stubborn jeans that wouldn't let her open her legs for him. "Oh God, hurry!"

She craned upward to lick his lips, and he kissed her again, easing a hand between their bodies, sliding it down, down, tangling his fingers in her pubic hair. She sobbed out a breath, raised her hips in encouragement and he delved lower, pushing between thighs that were almost clamped together. She started to shudder, her hands pulling at the hip band of his jeans, trying to free him.

"Make me come," she said. "Do it."

"I will," as he plunged his fingers into her.

"More, I need more."

But he stayed there for a maddening moment, loving the silky moisture against his fingertips, playing in her heat, absorbing the little shivers of her body.

"Matt!" she cried.

He eased off her, barely enough to free himself while one hand continued to play in her wetness. He jolted as his naked cock nudged at her opening, so eager for her he fumbled uncharacteristically as he slid his fingers out, pushed his cock inside. The fit was so snug he thought he wouldn't make it all the way in. But one thrust and he was there. *Fuuuuuuck.* He stopped to absorb the dizzying sensation of being one with her as she whimpered and gasped and gripped him. A blinding, heaven-hell moment. It was tight, so tight, having her thighs almost closed.

"God, you feel good," he gasp-groaned.

"So do you. Right there. Exactly there, exactly like that. Stay there. Fill me."

He tried, he really did, despite his cock demanding that he move into the age-old rhythm. He dropped his head to her shoulder, panting through the need. But it was no use. "Romy, I have to move. Just…oh God… once. Just once."

"Then do it, but hard, I want it hard. Fill me up, and up, and up." So he withdrew all the way, then pushed all the way in again. Stop. Counting in his head to try to control the animal urge. "That's sooo good," she moaned out, and he withdrew again but try though he did to regulate himself, when he plunged into her again he went so violently she shifted a foot along the floor. He stopped again, fearful that he'd been too rough but she didn't flinch and she didn't let go of him and he sure as hell wasn't letting go of her.

And then it was on. Ruthless. This was more than wanting her. He was claiming her as his so that whoever came after him could never own all of her. One, two, three, five, ten thrusts. Stuffing himself inside despite the constriction of her almost-closed legs, thankful for her drenching moisture but for which he could never have found his way. Whatever was happening, it was tighter, hotter, wilder than anything he'd ever experienced.

Missionary position. As vanilla as you could get, but this was *hot* vanilla. Hot and intense, like a secret flavor, hidden away for only him to taste.

All too soon the rush was there. He threw back his head, a "Gaaaaah" tearing from his throat as he tried to stop himself from coming and then he felt her inner muscles clamp. Another cry ripped out of him, like an endless death, in sync with her own, and he was coming and coming and didn't want to stop, never, ever stop. Didn't want to leave her heat. Never…ever…leave.

CHAPTER TEN

ROMY FLOATED BACK to earth slowly, breaths settling inhalation by exhalation, heart rate decelerating beat by beat.

She wanted the world to stop so she could keep savoring the feeling of Matt still inside her, his head nuzzled between her neck and her shoulder.

Her limbs felt heavy, her eyelids, too; she was warm and drowsy and replete.

She almost couldn't believe the things she'd said, telling him to go deeper, to stay there, to fill her. Unfiltered demands she couldn't imagine making of any other man. She felt a laugh burble up, because the moisture coating the inside of her thighs told her he'd taken her at her word and filled her all right.

He raised his head and looked down at her, and for a moment his eyes told her he could belong to her, and only her, forever. His eyes told her that he loved her.

She held her right hand to his face, and he turned his mouth to it, kissing her palm.

"Take it off," she said.

"Hmm?"

"The ring, take it off."

And in the time it took her to blink, the poignant tenderness she was so sure she'd seen in his eyes was gone and in its place was that other look, the one full of despair at what he'd done, what it meant. But that was just as fleeting, replaced by an emptiness so icy it made her shiver.

Funny how the springlike warmth their friendship had basked in for so long had transitioned so quickly into a season of extremes—the sear of summer, the frost of winter, no temperate zone.

Matt removed her hand from his face, withdrew from her body swift and hard, and stood. One hand hitched his underwear and jeans back into place. And it seemed they were back to square one: she may or may not be pregnant; he may or may not be interested; and sex was definitely not love.

Unutterably depressed, Romy moved more slowly—getting up off the floor, refastening her jeans, plucking the destruction that was her blue silk underwear off the floor and stuffing it out of sight in her back pocket because she didn't think he needed the reminder.

And then she fixed her eyes on him. "If you didn't really want me to take off the ring, what was the point of demanding that I tell you I want you, only you?"

He hunched a shoulder. "They're just…words."

"Just words," she repeated. "I see. Like love. And saying them during sex makes them meaningless?"

He took a step toward her. "Romy, I just—"

"No!" Pulling back.

"I wasn't going to— Ah, Jesus! I just— I want you to know that whatever applied before still applies, that's all."

"What does that mean?"

"Arrangements. The trust fund."

She took a slow, do-not-punch-him breath. "You know what? Go ahead and set up the trust fund—or not. I don't care. See your lawyer—or not. I don't care. I don't even care if you've been with fifteen women in the past month, as long as you give me a shout if you discover you've caught something nasty."

"I haven't."

"Caught anything? Good to know."

"*Been* with anyone. I'm monogamous on request, remember."

"I didn't request it."

"It was implied."

"Well, good for you, but like I said, I don't care."

"It's the truth."

"How many ways can I say I don't care?"

His jaw had tightened. "Just so you know, Romy, *I'll* care."

"You'll—?"

"If you're not monogamous, I'll fucking care."

"My, my, how *bourgeois*! But I suppose you have to have some guarantee that valuable trust fund won't be supporting another man's child, right?"

"I don't give a fuck about the trust fund."

"For someone who doesn't give a fuck about it, you talk about it a lot. But anyway, back to the new plan."

"We don't need a new plan."

"Sure we do, Matt, because whatever we've been doing for the past ten years isn't working for me anymore. For ten years, I've wanted you. And you've known it, and ignored it, because I guess you wanted me just as much as I wanted you but in a different *way*."

"Romy—"

"Please, just…let me say this. Think of us as actors in a movie, filming a scene that goes on way too long because nobody's prepared to call 'Cut.' You, our hero, are walled up in a castle tower surrounded by a moat. One by one, the best and strongest women in the kingdom have been diving into the moat and swimming across to the tower hoping to scale your impregnable wall, yet not one of them has made it inside.

"Enter the heroine of the piece—that's me, in case you're wondering. I've been assessing the structure of your tower for ten years, learning the makeup of the stone and waiting for the perfect moment to make my own attempt. And a window of opportunity opens, and I can see you framed in that window. So I jump into the moat and swim like crazy, but the water is murkier than I expected, choked with weeds, so it's hard work— so hard, I'm exhausted by the time I get to the tower. I don't care, though, because I've found a gap in the stonework at last, and even if it's not quite big enough to slip through, it's there, and I figure if I scrape and claw and gouge and dig, I'll find my way in. But it takes me a while to realize I've torn open my flesh trying to reach you, and my heart…my h-heart is on display. But when I look up to the window in that tower to ask you to open the drawbridge, because my heart needs you, and I know you can see me, clinging to the wall with my heart *bleeding*, Matt, bleeding for you…you turn away, even though you know I'll drown if I fall back into that moat."

"Stop, Romy."

But she wouldn't stop. She couldn't. "So I think we need to recut that scene, change it from a heart-wrenching drama into a fun comedy. Which is what we've done for the past ten years so it should be easy— all we really have to do is go back to being just friends. We even have a new window of opportunity, because you're here and I'm here, but this time, we need to stay here, as in *together*, so as to avoid any unfair accusations about who hasn't contacted whom in two weeks' time when I find out if I'm pregnant. My plan—let's call it Plan C—has two possible outcomes. One—I'm pregnant: we draw up new paperwork according to the level of friend zone success we've achieved. Two—I'm not pregnant: you go home and keep the hell out of my life." She offered him a wintry smile. "Deal?"

"No," he said, and picked up his duffel bag. "Contrary to what you seem to believe, I don't enjoy seeing you bleed, and whatever happens, Romy, you *will be in my life.*"

"I won't be in your life if you walk out that door, because I will never see you or speak to you again."

"That's not fair."

"Your definition of fair doesn't suit me. I've spent too long waiting for you to see me."

"I *do* see you, Romy."

"You see what you want to see, but I dare you to look harder. I *dare* you, Matt. Stay and play it out."

"Jesus!" he said, and picked up his overcoat.

Romy said nothing, did nothing. Even though she knew it would half kill her if he left.

And then he yelled, "Fuck." He glared at her. "FUCK!" He threw his overcoat and duffel bag across the room. "Fuck this, and fuck you for doing this to me."

Up went her chin. "You won't be fucking me, Matt, but other than that, I'll take your response as a yes."

CHAPTER ELEVEN

PLAN FUCKING C.

Matt gave his duffel bag, sitting innocently on the floor of the spare room to which he'd been relegated, a savage kick.

Fun comedy—so why wasn't he laughing?

Just friends—when it was fucking obvious that things had changed and he'd just made it fucking obvious to both of them the only way he could keep his hands off her was to do it from the other side of the fucking Atlantic!

He didn't know how to describe the way he was feeling. Like he desperately wanted to get away from her... yet he was terrified of not being with her. Like he was a wolf baying for a mate...but strangling himself to silence.

Excruciating. Agonizing. Confusing. Bewildering. All of those things together. With an overlay of panic that in two weeks' time she'd be pregnant...but maybe she wouldn't. That he couldn't control what happened, and couldn't even blame her for taking control out of his hands because he'd made a fucking mess of things in two countries!

Ha. To think he was in this latest mess all because of an *X* in an email. That pathetic *X* of a kiss, which was the way Romy signed off her emails to everyone—even that prick Lennie—and to which Matt had taken exception on the basis he wasn't going to start being an "everyone" to Romy after ten years' being number one with her!

And then to get to her apartment, and see Teague and...and resent him, in part because Teague was so damn perfect he *hadn't* slept with her when he'd had the chance?

Up came his hands, fingers rubbing at his forehead.

It was going to be a struggle to live with Romy in this tiny place for two weeks. She'd complained about noises through their old thin walls, but she'd hear his *thoughts* ticking in this apartment—and his thoughts were far from celibate. God help him if she came into this room, because there was barely room for the two of them to stand. He could probably cross it in three strides.

He took one long step past the single bed to test that theory, another, stretched his arms out and up and... stopped, mid-third-stride, because his hand had hit something.

He looked up and saw the mobile hanging from the ceiling—silver-and-white stars.

With a sense of foreboding, he turned a slow circle, taking in the freshly painted walls—a silvery gray with a scatter of white stars on one wall, the small rug on the floor with the same white stars on a gray background, a new white bureau against one wall.

Bump-bump-thump went his heart.

Because he was standing in the nursery.

He'd be *sleeping* in his baby's room.

He looked around the room again, soaking in the details. Typical of Romy to have the interior decorating under way before she was pregnant. Not that there was a lot to see other than the paint scheme and the star/moon theme. A lamp sitting on his bedside table—a full moon— was clearly intended for the baby. And the bureau, in white—that had baby clothes written all over it.

Curious, he went over to it and opened the top drawer. "Oh!" he breathed, as he saw the cache of tiny garments.

He lifted out a minuscule white cardigan, raised it to his face, rubbed the wool against his cheek. Soft as a cloud.

One by one, he opened the drawers, taking out all the other perfect things, holding them to his face, inhaling their pure scent. Three sleeper suits. Two pairs of knitted booties. A cap in white wool that matched the cardigan. Baby vests and leggings and tops. Wraps and rugs, a small fluffy towel. The tininess of each item as he carefully placed each item back in its spot squeezed his heart until he felt like it had been pushed up into his throat.

When only the little white cardigan remained, held against his chest, Romy knocked on the door. "Matt?" she asked. "Dinner will be ready in twenty minutes if you want to grab a shower."

He couldn't speak.

"Matthew?"

He took a moment to reel everything back in, hand rubbing his throat to ease the choking sensation there, and then forced out a "Got it."

Pause. "Are you okay?"

"I'm fine," he said. Because he *was* fine. Just fine.

If you didn't count that stinging at the back of his nose and the longing to tuck that tiny white cardigan under his T-shirt, right against his still-throbbing heart.

CHAPTER TWELVE

DINNER WAS...NOT GOOD.

Oh, not the steak and ale pie, which was as it always was, but the general atmosphere of *What the hell are we doing?* that had pervaded the flat.

Or perhaps the more accurate question was *What the hell am I doing?* because Romy knew very well she was the one who'd pitched them into this awkward hell. *She'd* wanted to have sex; *she'd* blackmailed him into staying; *she'd* positioned her heart ready for a trampling at the end of the two weeks when Matt left—as he would do, no matter which of her two scenarios came to pass.

She might have enticed him into having sex with her—twice, now—but the scalding truth was that she loved Matt and he didn't love her.

Love? Ha! He didn't even *like* her anymore, judging by his nonexistent dinner conversation. Her own dogged attempts at it—questions about Matt's flight, the chaos of Heathrow, the weather in San Francisco, his new business venture with Artie—were met with such headache-inducing vagueness, Romy almost wished for a return to the rage that had had her fearing he'd spontaneously combust before she'd shown him to the spare room and left him to froth at the mouth in peace.

When Matt opted to work in his room straight after dinner, Romy was relieved but also apprehensive. From tomorrow, she'd be at work during the days so the after-dinner hours would become important harbingers of the direction their relationship would take. Two weeks suddenly seemed a very short time to navigate their future as potential parents—it would be even shorter if they spent every possible minute of that time avoiding each other.

Romy didn't expect to fall into an easy sleep—and she didn't. Dreams of Matt had haunted her ever since she'd left San Francisco, and his presence in the flat acted on those dreams like an injection of steroids, supersizing them. The taste of his mouth, the feel of his hands, the way he fit inside her—they were all there. Right along with the things he'd said to her that night, which played in her head over and over... *If I said I wanted to see you on your knees for me, with my cock in your mouth, sucking... All that's of interest to me right now is if you're wet... I won't be satisfied until I'm buried inside you...*

No romance, not love words, but dear God, so indescribably, feverishly arousing she had to struggle not to go to him and tell him she was ready to suck anything he wanted her to suck.

Such a night left her ill prepared for seeing him in her kitchen the next morning. He'd gone for a run—as he always did—and looked so sweatily, deliciously scruffy as he scrambled eggs, she didn't trust herself not to lick him so she mumbled an apology about being late and left the flat without eating.

And despite lecturing herself half the day about Plan C's restrictions, when she arrived home that night all it took was one look at Matt sitting on her couch with a beer in his hand to knock her straight into the same state of salivating hunger in which she'd left that morning.

Matt's eyes locked with hers, the beer he'd been raising to his lips stalling halfway to its destination. He got to his feet as though hypnotized and the air thickened so that it would have taken a chain saw to cut through it— and Romy's briefcase slipped from her now-nerveless fingers and hit the floor, jarring them out of a trance that had nothing of friendship about it and everything about sex. Saved by the briefcase!

Romy blurted out something about chicken curry, Matt said he'd set the table, and they proceeded to keep out of each other's way until dinner was served.

They set the pattern that night for the rest of the week. A stilted conversation over dinner, followed by watching a movie on TV while occupying uncomfortably opposite-end-of-the-couch positions so as to avoid accidentally touching. Not exactly a return to their old friendship.

Matt gave up halfway through the movie, citing the need to check in with the manager he'd left in charge of his San Francisco hub, and Romy surrendered to a tension headache and went in search of painkillers and a restless night's sleep.

The next morning, when Romy cried upon waking at the prospect of seeing Matt in his running gear and actually touched the walls in the shower as she imagined soaping Matt's naked body, she knew she wasn't going to survive two weeks of living this way.

It was with considerable trepidation that she ventured out to the kitchen, where she found Matt looking hotter than sin. He plonked a plate of scrambled eggs and a mug of steaming coffee on the counter for her, giving her a rusty "Good morning" that melted her insides. Thankfully he then promptly took himself off for his turn in the bathroom, leaving her to choke down her breakfast around a mouthful of drool.

As she paused outside the flat and laid her palm on the wood of the door like she was trying to feel Matt through it, she knew a storm was brewing between them and it was going to either break or suffocate them.

Something was going to have to give, and give soon. The only question about it was which of them would be the catalyst.

Matt had no idea how he was going to reclaim his position in the friend zone when he was fucking Romy all night in his sleep and thinking about fucking her every moment of the day.

His solution was to distract himself by invading Artie's Wimbledon house. Annoyingly, he could think of only two business matters for them to discuss, and both were finalized by 11:20 a.m. on Matt's first day.

At that point, Matt decided he had no option but to confess to Artie that impending fatherhood was responsible for his earlier-than-expected arrival in London. He felt a surge of energy after getting that off his chest, and urged Artie to join him in some steam-releasing activities. But he was doomed to disappointment. Artie, never the most intrepid of adventurers, was uninterested in abseiling down the ArcelorMittal Orbit, rap jumping down a tower or kayaking on the Thames, and informed Matt that he got all the daredevilry he needed from his DIY obsession: in fact, his only recent hair-raising stunt had been making a birdhouse in his

mantuary—a.k.a. backyard shed—during which he'd
narrowly avoided slicing off an arm with a circular saw.

Which was when Matt had the brilliant idea of making his baby a crib. What better way of a) keeping
himself from going stir-crazy in that Romy-saturated
apartment, and b) demonstrating to Romy that he didn't
really think fatherhood was all about slinging money
at the kid?

By one o'clock, he and Artie had downloaded a de-
sign for a crib in a half-moon shape with cutout stars on
the sides to match Romy's nursery decor, ordered wood
and paint, familiarized themselves with the necessary
tools and were ready to blaze a home handyman trail
starting Tuesday morning.

And thus, the pattern of Matt's temporary life with
Romy was set.

He'd go for his morning run, then make and eat his
own breakfast. When Romy headed for the shower,
he'd scramble her eggs the way she always made them,
with mayonnaise, Parmesan and basil. She'd come to
the kitchen counter, they'd exchange a subdued "Good
morning" and he'd leave her to eat while he took his turn
in the bathroom. By the time he was done Romy would
have left for her Islington office and he'd be ready to
head to Artie's to get macho with the power tools. He'd
then be back at the apartment showering off man-cave
grime before Romy left her office at six o'clock for the
trip home.

When she arrived, Matt would be reduced to farcical
TV Sitcom Land, making use of anything readily available to hide his exhibitionist dick—his laptop, Romy's
London AZ guide, a cushion. If she'd had a damn pot
plant in the place he may even have snapped off a frond

and tied it around his groin! He'd get a reprieve while she cooked dinner, because she'd banned him from helping her in the kitchen on the—correct—grounds there wasn't enough room for the two of them.

They'd eat dinner while making inane conversation, then watch TV until the rigidity of perching as far away from her as possible without falling off the damn couch gave him an actual pain in the neck. At that point, he'd excuse himself to catch up on his San Francisco projects while the time zones were favorable, after which he'd dream about Romy all night and wonder if she was dreaming about him.

In other words, it was Hell. On. Earth.

And then, on Friday night, everything changed.

CHAPTER THIRTEEN

THE CRADLE WAS finished on Friday afternoon.

Artie was jubilant that they'd completed it with only one trip to the emergency room to get his forearm stitched.

Matt *had* been jubilant because he'd thought it looked fucking amazing…until he saw it in situ and by comparison to Romy's pristine paint job on the walls, realized it was in fact fucking crap.

He pictured Romy coming into the room in all her chic neatness and zeroing in on that drip of silver paint that he'd thought was unnoticeable but could now see would be visible from Jupiter using nothing but the naked eye. He envisioned her comparing his amateurish jigsaw-cut stars to the perfection of the ones painted on the wall. He imagined her waiting impatiently for Matt to leave London before she threw it out.

And then it sank in that he probably wouldn't *know* what she did with the damn cradle, because given the way things were going between them the chances of her inviting him anywhere near her for the rest of their lives seemed remote.

He thought back to what he'd said to her when she'd put Plan C to him—that whatever outcomes her Plan C covered, she'd be in his life no matter what. The truth was he needed that guarantee; it was what had driven all his decisions about Romy from the night he'd met her. Her, in his life somewhere.

And not the way they were at the moment. That wasn't having her in his life; that was *losing* her from his life—piece by piece, a little more every day. And it was going to have to stop.

He was going to fix whatever was wrong. Change the dynamic between them. There could be no more meaningless conversations over dinner. No struggling to keep their limbs separated on the couch. No more scheduling of morning showers to avoid contact. They had to have contact! They'd *always* had contact. Except for those four weeks after she'd flown home from San Francisco when he'd heard nothing from her, and he couldn't take another month like that. Nor could he wait another nine days to find out what sort of contact they'd have in the future. He had to know now, tonight.

Babies needed certainty, she'd told him. And he was ready to do his bit to guarantee their baby had it, via parents who would never give up on each other! If his gruesome parents could stay together for thirty years, he and Romy had to be able to manage some kind of longevity, didn't they?

Restless, he gave the cradle a gentle push with his fingertip to check the way it rocked on the nursery floor. Another push. Another. Picturing his tiny daughter in it.

He wondered if Romy had any names picked out. He kinda liked the name Rose… Similar to Romy, and yet…different. Pretty. Sweet. A little serious. He liked the idea of a serious kid.

Okay, it was a little crazy to be thinking so far ahead. The kid was still only a blastocyst, if she was here at all!

Still, he wondered what Romy would look like pregnant. As chic as ever. Beautiful.

He hoped she wouldn't get morning sickness. That would suck after all the pain she'd already been through. Morning sickness could be serious if you got it bad— like that type the Duchess of Cambridge got. She'd have to move in with her mother if she got that kind because it would be impossible to live alone and suffer like that. Or she could go into the hospital.

He'd better check out the hospital she'd chosen for the birth, now he thought of it. In case other serious shit happened. Blood pressure problems. Gestational diabetes…

Miscarriage. Twenty percent of women had miscarriages.

Or—hang on—did women still die in childbirth?

Jesus, he hadn't researched that one! He was going to have to look into it.

Because fuck.

Like…fuck.

No. Just no. Not going to happen.

He realized he'd stopped rocking the cradle and looked down at the sweaty palm he'd been gripping it with. He swallowed, breathed deeply, but the questions wouldn't leave him. Pregnancy, childbirth, the things that could go wrong. He was going to have a stroke thinking about this stuff when he was back in San Francisco.

Which…meant…ooooh. Holy shit! He was going to have to *not be* in San Francisco—he was going to have to be *here* for the next nine months to make sure nothing went wrong.

For a moment, he felt disorientated, and had to sit on the edge of the bed and breathe through it. Ha! Anyone would think he was having sympathy contractions nine months early!

Nine months. Living with Romy for nine months...

Was it possible?

Well, yeah! Perspective! He'd lived with her for three and a half years, hadn't he?

And all right, that was different. He hadn't even caught an accidental bathroom flash of Romy's body in all that time, and now he'd had sex with her twice and could visualize every damn inch of her skin. That made it a little harder to maintain a hands-off friendship.

Also, he was having a kid with her, for Christ's sake, so...so...ooooh. He was sleeping in the nursery, and he'd have to *get out* of the nursery so he and Romy could get the nursery finished, which meant there was only one place to sleep and that was with her.

He stared around the room, seeing nothing, as he assembled thoughts and then disassembled them. He wasn't flavor of the month with Romy—she'd told him sex was out of the question and she looked a lot like she wasn't intending to back down on that anytime soon. And he had no intention of backing down on it, either.

But...but...would it be so bad? If they put strict rules in place? It was only nine months, just until the baby arrived, and she could put together whatever legal documents she wanted to regulate the arrangement, couldn't she?

He had to shake his hands at that point to release some tension, then rub them on his jeans because his palms were sweaty again. Oh God. God! Whichever way you sliced it, this was a big deal. Huge! This was *not* a hookup. This was an affair. A real, bourgeois affair. He had to think this through. Maybe…maybe set the arguments out the way Romy did and try them on her tonight, easiest to hardest, no rushing his fences the way he usually did. He'd call it a Plan D.

He got up, went over to the cradle, set it rocking again, picturing a little tuft of red hair, a mini version of Romy's pursed duckbill lips.

He smiled. That kid was going to be *cute*!

CHAPTER FOURTEEN

MATT FIRED HIS opening salvo over their evening meal of spaghetti with ricotta, prosciutto and arugula pesto—"You look tired."

And okay, that statement wasn't going to set any woman's heart aflutter, but it was harder than he'd anticipated to think of something scintillating to say after five days of cold shoulder.

Romy didn't even look up from twirling a piece of spaghetti around her fork. "That's because I am."

Matt waited for her to finish eating that forkful, and tried again. "Tiredness is common when you're pregnant."

She paused, another forkful halfway to her mouth.

He gave her a weak smile. "I…er…read up on the symptoms, that month in San Francisco. Just…just in case."

The fork continued its journey in silence.

He cleared his throat. "So? Do you think you're… you know…*tired*?"

Aaand she laid down her fork. "I have no idea if I'm pregnant. If you're impatient for an answer because you're ready to call it quits and go home, however, I can grab a no out of the air for you. Or you could just *go*!"

"I'm not leaving, Romy," he said, which of course was exactly the point he'd been intending to work up to, but before he could elaborate she tossed her napkin on the table and stomped off to her bedroom.

Okay, that hadn't gone exactly as he'd planned. But he had a Plan E.

He cleared the table, stacked the dishwasher, sat at the dining table with his laptop, pretending to work in case she came out but in reality checking what was on TV because he knew Romy would be out eventually to watch it with him—she'd been making a point of *not* running away from him as though it were a badge of honor to suffer his company.

Sure enough, twenty minutes later she emerged in sweatpants and a loose T-shirt that screamed *I am in the friend zone* but which nevertheless set him on fire.

Out of the corner of his eye he watched her hesitate at the couch, then take up her usual position on the extreme right end, pick up the remote, turn on the TV and start changing channels at a rate of knots.

He took a couple of deep-but-silent breaths, adjusting his dick for the millionth time to try to give it a little extra room in his jeans, then he grabbed a beer for himself and a glass of water for Romy and made his way over to the couch. He deposited the drinks on the coffee table and took his allocated place on the extreme left.

Immediately, his penis eased out of the position he'd forced it into, making him squirm.

Romy looked at him, frowning. "What is it?"

"Just a twinge. In my…hip," he said, and grabbed the nearest cushion to thrust over his lap with a telepathic order to his dick to behave because he was *not* going to rush his fences!

"I've got some Deep Heat in the bathroom if you need something for it."

He almost burst out laughing at that. Deep Heat on his cock? That'd serve the bastard right. "No, I'll be… fine," he said, and he let himself look at her, really look at her, in a way he hadn't allowed himself for five days.

Every cell in his body seemed to vibrate with the need to touch her immediately. The idea of never touching her again was unendurable. And he didn't want to build an argument rationally—he just wanted her. Fast-tracked.

Okay, he was going to rush a fucking fence.

He threw his lap-covering cushion over the back of the couch. "Romy?"

She turned to him, her hand tightening on the remote. "Yes?"

"Stick a fork in me—I'm done."

CHAPTER FIFTEEN

"A WHAT?" Romy asked.

"A big, sharp fork. Or your teeth if you prefer."

She choked on the breath she'd been taking, coughed, wheezed, grabbed for the glass of water on the coffee table and took a massive gulp. *What* had he just said?

He grinned at her. "I can do kink, you know."

And she choked again, this time on the water, and coughed up half a lung.

"You okay?" Matt asked. "Maybe you need some of that Deep Heat."

Deep Heat? Yes! *Yes*, she needed deep heat. The deeper the better.

"But if you're trying to change my channel," he said, with a half laugh, "it's too late. It's preprogrammed."

"Wh-what?"

He gestured to the remote, and she looked down at it as though she'd never seen it before.

"Here," he said, taking it from her and pointing it at the TV. "Let's agree that the next channel switch we stick with no matter what."

But when he jabbed his finger on the remote and somehow found *The Proposal*, she wanted to snatch the remote off him and try again.

She and Matt had watched *The Proposal* together the night she and Teague had broken up. February 14, nine years ago to the day. Not that Matt would remember that. But it was etched in her mind as the date she finally accepted Matt didn't know she was equipped with boobs and a vagina.

"What is it about this movie and Valentine's Day?" Matt asked.

Blink of utter, *utter* insanity. "You *remember* watching this?"

"Well, yeah! *I* wasn't the one who drank a whole bottle of red wine on my own—my memory is unblotted. Now shh, we've already missed half of it." And he fixed his eyes on the screen while simultaneously reaching out a hand and yanking her close to him.

What the *hell* was going ooooon—dear God, he'd put a hand on her thigh.

She waited for him to move it. One…two…five…ten seconds… But his hand stayed where it was.

What was she supposed to do? Leave it there? She tried to think if she'd felt this hot and bothered in the old days when they'd watched a movie and he'd casually touched her, but her body had gone into free fall and there was only now. A deep, painful longing for him suffused her. She'd sit through anything as long as he kept his hand there—golf tournament, snooker, home shopping channel, even *The Proposal*.

"So," he said, his eyes still on the TV screen.

"Yes?" she breathed.

"Back to that fork…"

The fork. Ha! Stick a fork in *him*? Stick a fork in *her*! She was so done she was like a slab of overcooked pork crackling!

Matt hooted out a laugh as though he'd heard her thoughts, then gestured to the TV. "Do you remember this bit?"

She forced herself to focus on the screen. Ugh. "Unfortunately, yes. You made me get up and chant to the universe and dance around the living room."

"You didn't take much persuading."

"Red wine."

"Wanna have another go—without tripping over the coffee table this time?"

"Thank you, no."

"Then shh," he said, and as he refocused on the TV, he released his grip on her thigh and pulled her under his arm instead.

Romy kept watching the screen, conscious of the need to appear like she was just...well, breathing. Like a normal woman would breathe when she was jammed under the arm of a guy she was gagging for!

But she was struggling to take in anything, because she was seeing instead Valentine's Day evening nine years ago...

Matt and his date *du jour*, Kelsey, were going to a brasserie. Rafael and Veronica were at a diner because Rafael was broke and his pride wouldn't bend by so much as a quarter inch when it came to Veronica contributing funds toward their date nights. Romy, who'd been dating Teague for two chaste months, didn't know where Teague was taking her because it was a surprise, but she knew if she was ever going to sleep with him this was the night. She might have actually gone through with it, too, if he'd booked any old restaurant. But the moment she'd seen it was the exclusive, expensive Catch of the Day—which she'd been dying to try but couldn't afford—she'd had a crisis of conscience. Going to bed with Teague after such a meal would feel like a dinner-for-sex trade, and she liked him too much to go through with it. So she'd put her hand on his arm to stop him from entering the restaurant, and he'd given her his gentle, crooked smile and said, "It's okay, Romes. Apparently Valentine's Day breakups are almost as common as Valentine's Day engagements."

And they'd hugged, and she'd tearily rejected his what-the-hell-it's-Valentine's-Day offer of as much lobster and champagne as she could consume, and thirty minutes later Romy was back in the town house with a take-out pizza.

She'd been about to indulge in her first bite when Matt walked in, looked at the pizza in its box on the coffee table, at the glass of red wine beside it, and asked, "What's with the pizza?"

"Can't a girl order a pizza every now and then?"

"Not when the girl is you."

"I don't cook *every* night."

"Yes, Romy, you do. You're *obsessed* with cooking." And he'd swiped a slice, sampled it, grimaced, picked up the pizza and taken it to the kitchen, where he threw it in the garbage.

"I haven't eaten dinner!" she complained.

"If you want pizza, I'll take you to Vendetta's."

"It took so long to get into this dress I can't be bothered getting out of it just to go for pizza. The whole point of takeout was that I didn't *have* to."

"Yeah, I guess you do look overly trussed for a pizzeria."

"A real man wouldn't be deterred by a few buttons."

"*Any* man would be deterred by three million of the

things, so to save us both the effort…" dragging her off
the couch "…I'll make you something to eat instead."

He'd tugged her to the kitchen counter, got a beer for
himself, poured her a fresh glass of red, tapped the neck
of his bottle to her glass, taken a quick swig and started
gathering ingredients.

Recognizing the makings of Matt's infamous cheese,
bell pepper, chili and Henry's Hot Sauce omelet, Romy
had spared a mournful thought for her trashed pizza
capricciosa. But she knew Matt only made this partic-
ular omelet when someone was miserable—there was
something about hot sauce and egg that helped take
your mind off your troubles, he insisted, to everyone
else's disbelief—and so she'd said, "What happened?"
preparing to take one for the team and help him eat the
damn thing.

"Huh?" As he roughly chopped the pepper.

"Tonight. What happened with you and Kelsey?"

"Nothing." Shaking out a ton of chili flakes.

"Nothing as in…nothing?"

"What?" he said, distracted by cracking eggs into a
bowl and whisking enthusiastically. And then he paused
and looked at her. "Oh no, I don't mean *nothing* nothing.
I mean nothing *interesting.*"

He mixed the cheese, chili and pepper chunks into
the egg, tipped the mixture into the pan and pushed
it around with a spatula. A couple of minutes later he
scraped what looked like a lumpy red-and-beige splotch
onto a plate. Without ceremony, he poured the hot sauce
over it, threw a knife and fork on top and slid the plate
across the kitchen counter to her.

"Where's yours?" she asked, dismayed at the gargantuan size of the thing.

"Shit, *I* don't need to eat." He grabbed for his beer and took an enthusiastic swallow. "I had to eat Kelsey's dinner *and* mine because she's on a diet." Another slug of beer. "Fuuuucking hell, Romy—a diet!"

"She's a *cheerleader*, Matthew," Romy said, and shoved a valiant forkful into her mouth. She swallowed with some difficulty, then grabbed his beer off him, needing a sip to extinguish the flame in her throat. "She has to wear skimpy outfits, and people have to toss her in the air and…and things. You're the American—you know this stuff better than I do."

"So what?"

"Sooooo she can't eat like the rest of us—she has to keep her weight down."

"Oh. Yeah. I guess."

"And come on, you *know* girls don't look as good as Kelsey without a little self-deprivation."

"Who cares about looks?"

Romy choked on the bite of omelet she'd just taken. Took another sip of Matt's beer. "Name one nongorgeous girl you've been out with."

He grabbed his beer bottle back off her. "Names aren't important. And neither are looks."

"Ha ha."

"I'll qualify that—looks are a drawcard, but not if the rest of the person is annoying."

"Yeah, well, your problem is you're spoilt for choice. You get the pretty ones and the creative ones and the smart ones—all the ones."

"At least I don't get the nasty ones like you! Don't make me regret wasting the Omelet of Compassion on you, Romy."

Romy slowly lowered the laden fork that was halfway to her mouth. "What makes you think I'm in need of compassion?"

"Er...the pizza? Obvs!"

"Try again."

He ran a hand behind his neck. "Well, you're here, and Teague's not."

"How did you know I'd be here?"

Another rub of his neck. "I saw Teague at Flick's."

"Flick's? *Teague?*"

A look of annoyance crossed Matt's face. "It's not a den of iniquity you know, it's just a bar that happens to show films on Wednesday nights. They went anti-Valentine tonight with some godawful indie horror film. *Lots* of people were there."

"Yes, but Teague?"

"Why not Teague? At twenty-one he doesn't even need a fake ID, even if they could be bothered carding us, so—"

"It's not that! It's just... I don't know. It doesn't *seem* like him. It has a bit of a reputation."

"Oh, so Flick's is good enough for me but not for him? Yeah, well, he *was* there, halo and all! So I asked him why you weren't with him and he told me you two had called it quits."

"And you assumed I'd be in need of an omelet! Well, let me assure you the split was amicable." She pushed her plate away. "I promise you it wasn't worth leaving Kelsey unsatisfied."

"As it happens, smart-ass, we'd already done the satisfying stuff before dinner." He grinned. "*And* after. We were just out for a postcoital drink and the movie, and to be honest I was looking for an excuse to skip the film because there's a scene with an eyeball being chewed in *close-up*. Blech."

"I'm glad I didn't *completely* ruin your evening," she said drily.

"You don't *look* glad."

"Because you threw out my pizza!"

"Hey, I was going to take you out!"

"Oh, great—me eating and you watching!"

"Well, I... Sorry. I got a little ahead of myself with the pizza."

"That's because you always act first and think later. But since I don't need a babysitter, please take yourself back to Flick's."

"Don't make me go back there, Romy! I've got a DVD of *The Proposal* for us to watch instead—much better than a chewed eyeball. Kelsey said you'd like it and she's a film major so she'd know. She says it's perfect for V-Day."

"*Kelsey* suggested it?" Romy didn't know how to feel about not being considered a threat; she was *living* with Matt, after all!

"Come on, Romy, you know how squeamish I am. I can't take the eyeball. Don't make me go back there."

And so she'd laughed—of course!—and let him pour her more wine and put on the movie and tuck them both under a blanket on the couch. And then he'd poured her *more* wine, and made her do the chant-dance, followed by more wine...

And then came the scene with the ivory satin wedding dress and Romy had started to cry, and as though Matt had been waiting for exactly that, he'd scooped her up and sat her on his lap and patted her back and she'd snuggled against him.

Matt made stupid *It's all right, I've got you, You've still got me* murmurs into her hair, and even stupider than what he was saying was that she'd fallen asleep. Cradled on Matt's lap *she'd fallen asleep*! What a waste!

When she woke up, she was sprawled on Matt on the couch, and for the longest time she'd watched him sleep. Awake, he was always so sure of himself, and yet asleep there was something defenseless about him that made her want to hug him.

She'd felt an insane desire to take his face between her hands and rub her lips against his to see what it was that he gave to other women that he wouldn't give to her. It had shocked her, how much she wanted to do it, not only because it felt wrong to break up with one guy and kiss another all in the one night but because she hadn't allowed herself to think about Matt like that since that first night they'd met, when they'd *almost* kissed.

Whatever the reason, she'd sucked in a breath and the small noise woke him. For a moment, he'd stared at her, and then his eyes heated, and hooded. The hands that had been loosely crossed over her back tightened and he'd pulled her in close and she'd felt his erection.

Time stopped. She'd sensed rather than felt his heartbeat, steady and strong. Or maybe it was her own she was in tune with: it was telling her to kiss him, kiss him now because she might never get another chance.

"One thing I noticed last night…" he'd said, and she'd held her breath, dying to know. And then he'd grinned. "You look kind of like a troll when you cry."

"Oh, you…you bastard!" she'd exploded, whacking him in the chest and oofing her way off him.

"Hey, it's cute," he'd insisted, laughing at her disappearing back as she stomped to her room, where she told herself that she was to Matthew Carter what Teague Hamilton was to her. A friend you liked too much to love. A friend you needed in your life but not your bed. A friend, nothing more.

And now, so many years later, nothing had changed... and she still wanted him anyway...

"Hey—remember this bit?" Matt, giving her a nudge and bringing her back to the present. "Betty White trying to find Sandra Bullock's boobs in that dress. You started crying and said your boobs were too big, so you were going on a diet like Kelsey to shrink them."

"Yep, got it, thank you."

"And I had to lift you onto my lap and cuddle you."

"Aaaand you can shut up now."

"And I said I'd take a look at your boobs for you and give you an honest appraisal."

"Shut *up*, Matthew!"

"And you started undoing those three million buttons on your dress."

"Yes, I *remember*," she said, exasperated. "I also remember that you stopped me."

He looked at her, eyes heating. "I was a moron. How about I check your boobs now?"

Oh God, oh God, what did that mean? Fork. Done. No! If she asked about it, it would probably turn out to be something about barbecued steak! "Very funny."

"Except that I'm not laughing, Romy."

For one perilous minute, she vacillated...but then she remembered that her buttons *hadn't* been unbuttoned that Valentine's Day nine years ago, and she turned back to the television.

"I can hear you sniffling, Romy," Matt said. "Just saying."

"I'm not sniffling."

"Are you, you know, hormonal?"

She looked up at him. "Am I *what*?"

"When women fall pregnant, they get sort of emotional."

"Oh, they do, do they?"

"Apparently."

"Shut up, Matt. And stop reading up on pregnancy. You won't be here, so you don't need to know."

"I could be here. If you needed me. If you...wanted me."

She swallowed, letting that sink in. "You can barely fit in this flat *before* I'm fat."

"I fit better if I do this," he said, and lifted her onto his lap. "Just like old times, huh?"

Old times? Not quite, Romy thought.

"And yet not like old times, is it?" Matt said, as though reading her mind.

"No, not like old times," she said.

"You see, Romy," he said, "I have a feeling the old times aren't coming back. Which leaves us with a choice of either no times or new times. And I...I don't want no times."

Breathless. Wanting. "So what do new times look like?"

"That's something we'd need to work out."

"How do we do that?"

"I don't know yet. What I *do* know is I still want you. I know, also, that if you didn't want me, too, you'd be down the other end of the couch. So I have a suggestion, if you're interested in hearing it."

Could this be real? Oh God, she didn't know what to think.

"Romy?"

"What's the suggestion?"

"That I give myself to you for the night, and you do whatever you want to me and we see how we feel at the end. And if it's good…I stay. But I stay in your room with you."

"Do you mean that?"

"Cross my heart, hope to die."

"Just so you know, I'll help you with the dying part if this turns out to be a joke," she said, and tilted her head, closed her eyes, waiting for the kiss.

Long moment of…nothing. And then Matt spoke. "Er, Romy…? I think you've got the wrong idea."

CHAPTER SIXTEEN

HER EYES BOLTED OPEN. "I knew it! I'm going to get the carving knife!" she said, as she started pushing off his lap—but he held her tight.

"You don't need a knife if you want to kill me," he said. "All you need to do is say no. Because I'll drop dead if you don't take me within the next two minutes."

"Take…you? Oh, take *you*! You mean I'm in control."

"That's what I mean."

"But why?"

"Because you said no sex, therefore you have to be the one to reverse that order. Because I like the idea of being your slave. And because…I trust you with my body, like I've never trusted anyone before."

She felt tears prickle, as they always did when he said something that moved her.

He groaned. "Hey! Cut that out. Tears aren't sexy."

"But big tough guys who turn to putty when they see them are."

"I'm scared of trolls, that's all," he said.

"I don't think you're scared of anything, Matt."

He cupped her cheek in one hand and looked at her, very seriously. "I'm scared of *you*, Romy, and that's the truth," he said. And then he gave a shaky laugh. "But here's a hot tip to help you with my seduction—I'm an easy lay—it won't take much to make me come. So the floor is yours. Or the couch. Too bad there's not a chandelier or you could—"

"Shut up and kiss me," she said, leaping straight into the fray before anything could snatch the chance from her—and almost before she finished saying it his mouth was on hers, his tongue in her mouth.

One, two, three seconds—and he sat back, took her hand, put it over his heart. "Feel that?"

"Yes," she said. "It's banging like a drum."

"I am going to come so hard for you," he said.

Oh God, just hearing him say that! "I'm going to make you," she said. "But first, I'm going to kiss you and you're not going to kiss me back—this is just for me."

He kept himself still as she brought her mouth to his. First she kissed one corner, then the other.

When she pulled back to look at him, he touched her mouth and breathed out slowly. "That's just the start, right?" he said.

Instead of answering him, she leaned into him again, trailing tiny kisses between those two corners, sometimes letting her tongue slide between his lips, sometimes not.

She pulled back again, watching for his reaction. "Well?"

"Well," he said, and licked his lips. "Am I allowed to ask for more? Because I want more, Romy. I want you to kiss me all night."

And with a little cry of surrender, she planted her mouth over his. "Open," she said against his mouth. "Now you can kiss me back."

And obediently, he did, his tongue gliding deep and

wet into her mouth, seeming to touch everywhere at once. She swiveled on his lap to straddle him, her arms twining around his neck, knees digging into the back of the couch either side of his hips as she brought her body snugly against his. Her hips moved back and forth, and so did his, as if their bodies were already planning to take over the show. He felt so good there, *her* toy now, and the thought that she could do whatever she wanted to him was an exhilarating one, even if all she really wanted to do was strip off their clothes and impale herself on him.

But she remembered how in San Francisco, when she was climbing the stairs, she'd wished she could be memorable for him, and so she forced herself to slow down, to throttle back. She would tell him what to do to her, because he wanted her to do that, he *trusted* her to do that—and being the one he trusted was already something memorable.

Her hands went to the hem of her T-shirt. "Do you know what I want you to do to me when I take this T-shirt off?" she asked.

"Tell me."

"I want your hands on my breasts. And then your mouth. I want you to coax my nipples out, to not stop until you do."

"Oh Jesus," he groaned. "I am so up for that."

She laughed, low and soft, and scooting back as far as she could on his lap, lifted her T-shirt up and off. Lowering her arms to her sides, she lifted her chin. Displaying the wares. Watching his eyes drop to her chest. Seeing him swallow hard. Her breasts seemed to swell from the heat in his eyes, begging to be released from the confines of her bra.

"Well?" she said.

"Well," Matt said fervently. "I could drool a fucking river looking at you."

"Hands. On me."

And as he raised his hands, placed them gently over her covered breasts and her heart gave a savage leap. He raising smiling eyes to hers and she knew he'd felt it.

He started to move his hands in circles over the white mesh of her bra, and her nipples tingled as though getting ready for him. One firm squeeze, and he pulled his hands back but only far enough for his fingertips to take over the work, drawing the lightest of circles around her areolae, which were on clear display through the mesh of her bra.

She huffed out a shuddering breath, so hot for him she thought she might scream. One more circle, another, another, each one infinitesimally smaller than the last, heading inward to his twin targets.

She squirmed on his lap, frustrated, and the way he laughed low in his throat told her he knew exactly what he was doing to her. Well, of course he knew!

But she wasn't entirely clueless, either, and when she made a little figure eight on his lap with her backside, using her hips to propel her, he actually gasped, his cock doing an involuntary lunge upward against her heat. "Ride me if you want, Romy. Do anything to me. Ask anything of me."

"Then…then I want your fingers on my nipples, right on them, right now, rubbing," she said.

"Your wish…my command," he breathed out, and used two fingers to rub each nipple through the white mesh. "Tell me when I can use my mouth."

A deep, drawn-out moan of a "Now" had him going

straight to the job, holding her breasts in his hands and bending forward to lick around one areola, then the other, moving back and forth, back and forth again and again, before shifting to her nipples and using the flat of his tongue to lick her like an ice cream, then the tip to stab into the centers.

"Soooo gooood," she sighed.

"Don't I know it," he groaned, and gave each nipple a lightly sucking kiss.

"Take off my bra," she said. "I need you to touch me properly."

"How about I do it like this?" he said, and peeled the cups of her bra down. He leaned back to look at them, licking his lips as though he could taste her. "Ahhhh, God, it's a crime, how sexy you are."

She slipped her hands under his T-shirt, ran the palms up his chest. "You feel so hot."

"I am hot. Hot for you. Hot and hungry and ready."

She pulled her hands free, sat back to give him room. "Then take off your T-shirt."

He pulled it up and off lightning fast. "Romy, please touch me," he said. "Please."

She put her hands over his pecs, rested them there for long seconds, absorbing the thud of his heart and then moving her hands in the slow circles he'd used on her. "Are your nipples as sensitive as mine?" she asked.

"Find out," he said, and she moved her hands, softly, delicately circling them with her fingertips.

"Yes," she said. "They're hard. Oh, I wish you could feel mine."

"Say the word and I'll get back to work."

"First, I want to do this," she said, and leaned in so

that her breasts were only just touching his chest. She closed her eyes, lost in the moment. "Oh, I like that."

He bucked against her, as though jolted by a burst of uncontainable energy.

"Don't," she ordered, even though she loved it. "Stay still and let me do this. It feels so wonderful." And it did, her skin against his, the crunch of his hair against her nipples, the graze of his own small nipples against her.

"Are you trying to torture me, Romy?"

"What do you mean?"

"Do you know how hard it is for me to wait?"

"Yes, because I've waited ten years for you, wanting this."

"So you're punishing me?"

"No," she said. "No, never. I would never hurt you. I want to give you everything." For an instant, she sensed a withdrawal in him, and the next moment his hands were in her hair, his forehead pressed to hers.

"Not those words tonight," he said.

"Why not, when I mean them?"

He released her, eased back, not answering. "Come on, get rough with me. I want you to fuck my brains out and make me beg."

Her hips moved, her core sliding over him, back and forth. "Does it feel good to have me do that?"

"Yes, you know it does—you can feel how hard I am."

"So say the words. Tell me exactly. I like it when you say the words to me."

He smiled again, a sexy curve of mouth. "It feels so good when you ride my cock. You make me so big and hard, I can't wait to be in you. I want to make you wet. I want to fill you up. I want to do you fast and slow and make you come all night."

"Yes," she panted, restless, seeking.

"So can I?"

"Not until you make my nipples come out. Undo my bra."

Swiftly, he undid the back clasp of her bra and stripped it from her.

"Get to work," she commanded.

He recupped her breasts with his hands, going straight for the nipples now, thumbing them gently, then harder, then pinching them between thumb and forefinger.

The air was full of small sounds. Sighs and moans and gasped-out breaths and tiny sucking sounds, rasps from his jeans against her as she writhed on his lap.

"Now your mouth," she said. "Lick them. Suck them. Say again you'll do anything, but this time I want to know it's only for me, no other woman."

"Only for you, Romy. Only ever for you will I do what I'm told, always you, only you, forever."

She closed her eyes, surprised that the words brought her pain, and he seemed to take that as his cue to increase the pressure because he went hard at her now, hands squeezing her breasts, settling in to suck on her, focused on only one, going hard, hard, hard, as though he were starving for her, so that she was arching her back and dragging his head closer and tighter. The intensity hovered just short of pain.

She let out a low, keening cry, and he went crazy, his sucking almost frenzied. And unbelievably, with one last, long, luxurious suck, her nipple popped out into his mouth.

He pulled back, looked at it and she felt herself flame.

"I am so horny," he said, low and hoarse, as his fingers went to where his mouth had been, pinching and rolling. "I'm scared I might actually come." And he shuddered as though to underscore the truth of it.

"Suck me again," she said, and he bent his head and kept sucking, this time using his fingers on the other nipple as though to prepare it. And then with one final light bite, he switched sides, using the same technique, the same firm suction, the same concentration, and it happened fast his time, the nipple suckled into his mouth, eager and ready.

"Now," she said. "Now. I need you inside me now."

"Not yet," he begged, as he continued to lash one nipple with his tongue, twirl the other with his fingers, pinching, rolling, squeezing.

"Now," she said again.

"One minute more," he begged, and latched onto her nipple, sucking and sucking until she was shifting on his lap, whimpering, panting.

"I'm going to come if you keep going!" she cried.

"Good."

"No!" she said, and pushed against him so that she tumbled backward and would have fallen to the floor if he hadn't caught her hips, pulled her up, held her steady.

"You are driving me fucking wild, Romy," he said.

Their eyes clashed, warred. She undulated on his lap and a look of triumph came into her face. "Then kiss me, show me," she said, and he dragged her in, lunging his cock so high and tight against her she almost wished he'd take over, roll her under him and jam his cock into her. His mouth landed on hers, his tongue thrusting as though he were fucking her mouth, and she lost all sense of time and space until there was only heat and lust and musk.

Her slave. He really was her slave.

"Let me have you, Romy," he said against her mouth, between deep, drugging kisses. "Let me have you now."

And she was off his lap, dragging him up after her, kissing him again as her hands went for his jeans. Unzipping, hands diving, gripping him, squeezing him. "I want to see you naked," she said, and stepping back, she flicked a hand at his jeans. "Get them the fuck off."

"You bet," he said, and while he kicked his way free of his jeans and all but tore off his boxer briefs, she stripped off her sweatpants, her underwear.

And then she stopped to breathe before lowering herself onto the couch, where she laid herself out like a feast, and when he looked at her she felt a surge of power that this man, of all the men in the world, would want to be hers even for a fleeting moment.

As Matt looked at her, so confident on the couch, tenderness almost blinded him. She'd asked him to tell her he'd do anything only for her, no other woman.

To him it seemed so obvious, it didn't need to be said. Ten years of running only to her, ten years of doing whatever she asked. Even the fact that she'd asked him to take her, that night in San Francisco, the first time she'd ever outright asked, was proof. Because he'd held himself so rigidly back from her for so long—and yet he'd obeyed her. *Of course* he had. Here in London, too. It wasn't in him to deny her what she wanted. She'd always belonged to him, in every way but this—and now she was claiming this, too. Did she not see that he always would have done this for her if she'd asked? That he'd already done everything he could think of to keep her with him, even when the only way he could think of was to deny himself this final piece?

His body one giant throb straining toward her, held back only because he'd put himself at her command and she was reveling in her power over him.

Her silky light brown hair was spread out above her head. One arm was crooked beneath her head, the other stretching up the back of the couch, her hand flopping over the back of it. Creamy skin. Sleepy eyes. Mouth swollen from his kisses. Those small pink nipples, hard and impudent and all the more amazing because he'd had to work for them, and because she'd demanded he work hard. The tiny tangle of hair at the apex of her thighs, which made him want to fall to his knees and beg her to open her legs for him.

As though she'd divined that unspoken need, she spread her legs so that one foot was on the couch, the other on the floor. Like she was saying: yours.

"Ah, Romy," he said looking down at her. The moment felt too big for words, the air heavy with the promise of something special.

"Come," she said.

And slowly, he lowered himself on top of her, waiting for her arms to enclose him, folding his own tightly around her at the same time as he closed his eyes—the better to sharpen the moment. He stayed like that, quiet and still, for the longest time, absorbing her.

When he opened his eyes, it was to find her waiting for him. She strained up to kiss his mouth, deep and soft, and she kept kissing him as he slowly, so very slowly, entered her.

He stopped when he was all the way in, wanting to remember this moment because surely sex could never be so blissfully perfect again. And then he moved. Out, in, out, keeping it slow and rhythmic so she knew exactly what to expect.

Over and over he entered her, and she kept her mouth on his all the while. He wanted to take forever, wanted to immerse himself in the sound of sex, the arousing smell of her, the taste of her mouth, the pant of her quickened breaths, the feel of those delicious little nipples poking against his chest, the strength of her inner thighs gripping the outside of his as though she'd never let him go. But his cock was trying to slip the leash, desperate for the finale, and his orgasm was building, grabbing at him despite his efforts to slow it down.

Not yet, not...yet. He ground out the words in his head, but he knew it was a stroke or two only away. His breaths were heaving so much, he had to move his mouth off hers, gulping in air as his hips rubbed against hers. *Oh God, not yet, I want more.*

And then Romy's whole body went stiff. A gasp, and cry, her wet heat tightening around him as he sucked against her neck, then licked, then sucked, then licked.

"Let me say it, Matt," she said.

Oh God, he knew. Knew what she wanted. He shook his head, no. *No! Let me just have this.*

"I have to say it, Matt."

Panic. "No!" Aloud? In his head? "No, no, no, please no, just let me, let me, Romy."

But it was out of his control. Push, push, push, push, his body inside hers, owned. Her heart was thumping in time with his, the smell of her wrapping around him as surely as her arms. *Oh, please, no.*

"I love you, Matt," she cried, and the words pushed him over the edge so that he abandoned himself to the waves. "I love you, Matt. I love you, love you, love you. Ahhhhhhhh, I love you. Love."

Silence.

Full. Heavy. Lost.

His arms unwrapping, his mind unraveling, his body shivering.

He eased himself up over her, hands on either side of her, looked down into her face and all he could think was, *No, please don't say it*, even though it was too late.

She watched him. Boldly, unwavering, unapologetic.

Was she expecting him to say something? Because he had nothing to say.

He moved off her, stood, located his jeans and put them on. Found his T-shirt, dragged it over his head. He was covered, but he still felt exposed.

Romy sat up without taking her eyes off him. "What is it, Matt?"

"You know."

"Just words. Three little words."

"You promised not to say them, that night in San Francisco. You told me you refused to love me."

"And yet you knew I did."

"But you didn't tell me, you didn't say it. And then… Ah Jesus. You said them like that. At that…that moment. That's not love, Romy."

"So if I'd said them over dinner, that'd be different? You'd have *welcomed* them over dinner?"

He shifted his shoulders. He felt worn out. Exhausted. "Well, doesn't matter, does it, because now I've heard them. So…thanks. I guess." He gave a throat-clearing cough, wanting his voice to be steady. "I'm going to catch up with Teague tonight, have a few beers."

More silence. Stretching, as she watched him.

Another clear of his throat. "You know, Teague…"

"Yes, I know Teague," she said. "Your friend. The man I'm supposed to be with. *That* Teague."

"He and I…" Pause. "We're going to…" Pause. "I'm… due there soon."

"And is it going to be an all-nighter with Teague?"

"Maybe."

"You asked me for tonight, Matt. All night."

Again, his shoulders shifted. "Plans change."

She sighed as at last she got off the couch. "Okay then, we understand each other," she said, and put on her sweatpants, her T-shirt—not hurrying.

"The whole…whole friend thing. We all need to get back to that. You. Me. Teague."

She sighed again. "You don't have to explain yourself to me, Matt. We…you and I… I guess we sorted out those 'new times' we were curious about, so we're good. On the same page."

"Are we?"

"Well, maybe the same book, different chapters. You gave yourself to me to do with what I wanted, I did what I wanted and now we both know what's what, how we feel."

"Romy—"

"I love you and want to have sex with you because of that. You want to have sex with me, but don't want to love me because of that. I guess that translates into you being at chapter five while I'm up to chapter twenty-five. But whereas I know I want to finish the book, you're bored with it and want to move on to a different story."

"That's not— I mean—"

"What? Did I misinterpret something?"

Matt tried to figure out how to say his feelings were

more complicated than that, but when he thought of all the plans he'd made for himself just a few hours ago, all he could come up with was: "I need you, Romy."

She sucked in a breath, like he'd hurt her. "Yes, I think I know that. But I need you all the way, no secrets, no fears. And that's different from the way you need me." She smiled, with a roll of her eyes that managed to be both dismissive and defensively dramatic. "I shouldn't have called it love, I know, when you can't feel it, when you don't…don't know the…the *agony* of it. And it *is* agony, it really is. But I'm running out of nouns and adjectives, so you might have to give me some help there. I mean, we're not friends anymore, are we? I haven't been feeling much of a sense of camaraderie this week. I don't think what we just did was affectionate. We're not really having a casual fling because you're not using a condom the way you always do. So if you don't want it to be love, I don't know… Fuck buddies perhaps? Except that I've broken the cardinal rule so that's obsolete. How about ex-hookup?" She ran her hand over her hair, smoothing a tangle. "How strange that I thought I was different, being the only female you weren't interested in fucking…and now I'm just like all the others. Right down to telling you I love you at the peak of an orgasm, like the worst cliché. But I understand it now, Matt. I understand all those women who choose that moment to do it. It's that gap in the tower wall, you see. We can't help saying it at that moment because you make us feel so close to you, like we really could slip inside and find you. I even know why they don't want to be your friend at the end—because it hurts to see you and not have you. And you know what? I'm glad I'm not different. I never *wanted* to be different. I *want* to love you. And *I* don't want to be your friend at the end, either."

She picked up her underwear and headed for her bedroom, saying over her shoulder, "Better get your skates on or you won't make it to Park Lane by eleven."

Ten minutes later, Matt found himself outside Romy's flat, leaning against the wall like a drunk, one hand over his eyes. The agony of love. She'd called it agony, what she felt for him. He stood there for a full five minutes, battling the stinging at the back of his nose he was starting to get used to.

And then he took a deep breath, and headed out into the night.

CHAPTER SEVENTEEN

ROMY SPENT THE first half of the night lying in bed, re-living Matt's reaction to her grand declaration of love—which was to look at her as though she'd stabbed him straight through the heart he professed not to have.

The second half of the night she spent pacing through the flat, wondering what she could expect from Matt when he eventually returned.

When there was no sign of him by nine o'clock, she switched to wondering *if* he'd return.

By eleven o'clock, she was convinced he wouldn't.

She'd gone to his room many times, hesitating outside, knowing one quick peek would tell her if he'd taken his duffel bag. But she hadn't been able to bring herself to open the door, instead hurrying to the kitchen to distract herself by making coffee—and for her to make coffee instead of tea was a true indicator that her state of mind was unsound.

By noon she'd drunk so much coffee she was totally wired—which she figured explained the sudden grip of terror that convinced her Matt was lying dead in an alley.

At one o'clock, she pulled up his number, ready to call him despite the fact that last night she'd told him he didn't have to explain himself to her…and then made more coffee instead.

At two o'clock, she had the brilliant idea of calling Teague to find out what he knew, and when he answered on the third ring she almost collapsed with relief.

"T-Teague?" she stammered.

"Romes!" he said. "Let me guess—you're calling to tell me all is well in the land of the lovers so I can stop worrying about you."

"You'd know more about that than me."

"Er…not following."

"Is Matt—? Did Matt—? Oh!"

"Still not following."

"Matt said he was spending the night with you, but… he didn't. Of course he didn't."

"Oh. Er…"

"Don't," she said. "Please don't cover for him. There's no need. It's none of my business where he spends his nights. I'm not his girlfriend. And that…that's not what's worrying me. It's just…you know how reckless he is, and I keep expecting to hear he's BASE jumped off The Shard and broken his neck or something, so—"

"Hang on, hang *on*! He's lying to you about where he's going, you're checking up on him and you're telling me you're not his girlfriend?"

"He doesn't have those."

"Well, you're not just friends if that's how you're both carrying on."

"We're not friends at all anymore, it seems."

"Oh, Romy, you two were never friends. Look, much as it pains me to do this, let me give you some advice— stop giving him so much rope, because he'll keep hanging himself with it."

"Rope?"

"Stop letting him come and go in your life as he pleases, see any woman he wants, do anything he likes. He doesn't want that freedom—not from you. Deep down, he wants you to give him boundaries."

"I don't…understand."

"Matt's problem is nobody ever reins him in. Not his friends, because we like him exactly the way he is—fast and brilliant. Not the women he attracts just by breathing, because they'd give him anything he asks for—which sucks, by the way, for guys like me who don't get a look-in when he's around. As for his parents—well, they don't want to rein *themselves* in let alone anyone else, and I don't think they'll be happy until they corrupt him absolutely."

"I don't—? His parents? I've never met them."

"Now you see, that's interesting. Ask him why. And while you're at it, *tell him* what you want from him, how you feel, lay it on the line—"

"Oh, Teague, I already told him how I feel." She closed her eyes as the heat of humiliation flooded her. "Last night I told him I loved him."

"Aaand it all makes sense. You told him—he ran away."

"What am I going to do?"

"Tell him again. Keep telling him. Keep showing him, too, but you've been showing him forever, so I have a feeling it's the telling that's going to get him."

"He doesn't like being told. I knew that, and I told him anyway."

"He'll hear it, from you he'll hear it, but you'll have to make him hear it, and hear it, and hear it, because he won't believe it."

"And if I lose him for good?"

"Then at least it'll be an outcome, won't it? For you, if not for him. You can't keep limping around the edges of a relationship with him, Romy. If he really won't step up to the plate, it's time he let you go so you can find someone else. Someone who…who wants all of you, not just the parts Matt will spare."

"He'll say no—he won't step up."

"Then let him say no, and let him go. Look, just… think about it, okay?"

"Okay, I'll think about it…I think."

Teague laugh/sighed. "Okay, but while you're thinking about thinking about it, consider that every time you've needed him he's come running—and when I say running, I mean sprinting. You know, the night you and I broke up and I saw him at Flick's and told him we were through, he was out the door faster than a speeding bullet—"

"He hates being compared to superheroes."

"Then he should stop trying to save you. The point is, I was sure he was off to get the girl that night—but here you are, ten years later, still limping along the edges."

"Don't you think that means it's not supposed to be that way for us?"

"No, I think it means he's terrified. You're *different* for him, Romy."

"That's just it—I'm not different. I'm like everyone else who wants him but can't have him."

"I'm not talking about sex, except insofar as it took him ten years to get around to it with you—which *is*, in fact, the difference. He's scared to death of you, scared a wrong move will lose you, scared of his…his need for you to see him the way you see him. Because I'm telling you, he may not like you supersizing his heroism but he also kind of lives for it. He wants to be a hero for you, but deep down he won't believe he can be. He's scared—but don't you be scared, too, or you'll both still be limping around those edges when you're ninety. Anyway, enough Truth or Dare." He took a breath. "I'll tell you what I'll do. I'll text him, make sure he's alive, and then I'll text you so you can use your brain for more productive things than worrying about the idiot."

Romy received the "all clear" text from Teague half an hour later, but by four o'clock there was still no sign of Matt.

The time had come to make sure he hadn't moved out. Without hesitation this time, she opened the door to his room, walked boldly in…and her jaw dropped at the sight of a silver cradle in the shape of a half-moon.

She walked over to it, not quite believing it was real even though its slightly mangled cutout stars smacked of a DIY project so it was hardly a celestial gift beamed out of nowhere.

This was what Matt had been doing all week while she was at work? Not plotting a tech takeover of the world, but making his baby a cradle?

She blinked in disbelief as she ran her fingertips over the wood. As she gave it a little rock. And then she couldn't seem to stop blinking—not in disbelief anymore, but because tears had formed in her eyes. Everything about the wonky cradle moved her unbearably. Because she knew in that blinding, wrenching, heart-shattering moment that she'd gotten something very wrong about Matt and his motivations. He'd suggested giving her his sperm not as a favor to her, not to be a godfather, but because he wanted a baby. He'd wanted, specifically, *her* baby. He'd flown to London to stop her from finding a different donor because he *loved* their baby. He'd loved it then, when it didn't exist, and he loved it now when it *still* might not exist. He loved it even though he'd probably never be able to say the words.

And *she* loved *him*—so much in that moment she would have gladly cut out her heart and given it to him on a plate made of her own soul, painted not black but silver and white, to match the priceless, utterly wonderful gift he'd made for their child.

She put both her hands over her belly. "Please be there, my little one," she whispered. "For your daddy, if not for me, because whether or not he knows it, he needs you."

CHAPTER EIGHTEEN

THERE WAS NO sign of Romy when Matt opened the door at 7 p.m.—not even a wisp of aromatic steam coming out of the kitchen, which was where she'd normally be at this time of night.

He experienced a short burst of relief, followed almost immediately by a surge of panic.

But then he heard his name, "Matt?" called out like a question from her bedroom and the panic receded… and then surged right back, because he had no idea what he was going to do.

He'd had a turbulent night and a torturous day wandering the city, trying to work out why Romy's *I love you* was different from every other *I love you* he'd ever heard even though it *wasn't* different, why it made him want to stay instead of leave, why leaving therefore was exactly what he should do and why he needed to stay anyway.

Yeah, like any of *that* made sense.

"Matt?" she called again.

He opened his mouth to say yes, it was him, but when no sound emerged, he closed it.

And then she was there, in the room with him, smiling as though nothing had happened last night. "I'm glad you're back. I need you," she said, and walked over to him holding out something he accepted by reflex.

"Can you put that in for me?" she asked, and when he looked down at his hand he saw it was an earring. "The left ear is always tricky, as you know."

Of all the openings Romy could have given him after last night, this was about as far from his imaginings as it was possible to get.

"Matt?" she prompted when he stood there like his own mummified remains, and she moved closer so that their bodies were almost touching. And God, how he wanted to touch her, even if it was only her ear. He wanted to beg her not to hate him. He needed her to put her arms around him and hold on to him. He felt so lonely for her, which didn't make sense when she was standing in front of him.

She tilted her head as trustingly as ever, moving her hair out of the way. He started to put the spike of the earring through her lobe, but his fingers were trembling so much it took three attempts. "You need to get it repierced," he said—an excuse for his clumsiness.

She offered him a tremulous smile. "I'll get you a needle and you can do it for me."

"Needles hurt." He touched her cheek with his fingertips. "And I don't want to hurt you, Romy."

"So *don't* hurt me." Her smile failed. "Please don't, Matt."

He choked on what might have been a sob if he knew how to cry, and stepped back out of harm's way. And that's when he noticed she was wearing a silk dress and high heels. Her hair had been styled, her makeup carefully applied and there was a hint of Chanel in the air.

"You're going out," he said.

He saw her physically pull herself together. "My monthly dinner with my parents, which I completely forgot about until Mum called me this afternoon!" Pause, as she reapplied her smile. "If you want to come, I can wait a few minutes…?"

He swallowed. Shook his head. Took another step back, then stepped forward again because that was just too pathetic. What was he scared of—that she'd *love* him to death?

She took a gusty breath. "Okay then. I've left some menus on the kitchen counter—several restaurants nearby do home delivery. Or…or maybe you already have plans?" Pause, during which she very clearly braced while he said nothing. "Well, whatever. If you stay in and want to…to talk, about…about anything, I don't expect to be out too late."

She started to move past him but he stopped her. "Is Teague going to be there?"

"No."

"Has he met your parents, Romy?"

"Yes, he's been to a few of these dinners."

"So why did *I* never meet them on one of my trips?"

She looked at him for a long moment. He got the feeling she was choosing and discarding words. Then she shrugged and said simply: "Because it didn't work out that way."

"Why didn't it?" he pushed, because he wanted to know. Maybe it would help him to make sense of their relationship.

"Because we've never had the kind of…of friendship that would make such a meeting easy."

"How can he have been enough of a friend to meet them but not me?"

"Probably the same reason you took Teague home to meet your parents but not me."

"That's...different."

"Yes, and you and I are different from me and Teague or you and Teague. Or you and Veronica and Rafael and Artie and— Oh, Matt, can't you see that we're not friends in the same way? That we never were? We *couldn't* be, because I—" She broke off. Shook her head. "Look, you don't want to hear it and I'm late—I really have to go."

She tried to move past him again—again he stopped her.

"Do they know about me, Romy?"

"My parents? Yes. They know we were friends in college. They know we've been friends ever since. They know you're staying here. They want to meet you because they know about the sperm—in fact they half expect you to come with me tonight."

"Have you told them how we did it? The sperm? That it wasn't—"

"No. There didn't seem to be much point since... Well, let's just say I discuss almost everything with my parents, but not one-night stands."

"Three nights."

"Different number, same principle."

His head felt like it might explode. "I think..." Trailing off. Clearing his throat. "Doesn't matter. Have a nice time at— Where did you say you were going?"

"Petit Diable. I took you there last year, when I was dating the sous chef, Jules."

"Oh, Jules—yeah, I remember."

"That was the time you met Poppy." She took her overcoat off the coat stand by the door and slipped it on. "And you insisted Jules and I meet up with the two of you for brunch."

"Why are you mentioning that, Romy?"

She faced him. "Because I've decided there are some things I won't do anymore. Like having brunch or lunch or dinner or drinks or anything else with you and your latest hookup. I don't want to talk to them on the phone or see them on video calls or read their emails. I just... don't."

"You have to do that, Romy! I need you there."

"Why?"

"Stops them giving me ultimatums. Them, or you. I have to...to show them—"

"That I'm not a threat? Well, that makes sense. They meet me, they can tell what I mean to you and all is well in your world and theirs."

"I choose you. I *always* choose you."

She shook her head at him sadly. "Oh, Matt, that's not a choice. That's called having your cake and eating it, too. And I'm tired of being the vanilla sponge you refresh your palate with between bites of chocolate gâteau. I want to be the gâteau."

"That's not fair, Romy. I've never—"

"Don't!" She held up a hand. "It doesn't matter, Matt. It really doesn't." She opened the door, but stopped on the threshold, turned back. "You said something last night about old times and new times. Well, I'll find a way to accept that the new times are over—San Francisco, last night, done. But in return, you need to know that what we've had for the past ten years has to be over, too, because I'm not going back to the old times. I *can't* go back, even if what we end up with is nothing."

* * *

I can't go back, even if what we end up with is nothing.

Matt knew what nothing felt like—it was how he'd describe those four weeks after Romy had left San Francisco. But even in the midst of the full-blown freak-out that separation had brought on, he'd known that if he could have gone back and changed what had happened that night, he wouldn't have done it.

The miracle was that he'd held himself back from her for so long. He should have known he'd wouldn't be able to keep his hands off her forever. It was what he was like, the real him, not the hero she thought he was. *Of course* he was going to engineer a way to have her eventually. And the fact that she'd been the one to suggest that infamous Plan B didn't change it. He'd leaped at Plan B! And look what had happened when her email had arrived—not pregnant, off the hook! He should have taken that as a sign that it wasn't meant to be—instead he'd thrown the first things to come to hand in his duffel, snatched up his passport and headed for the airport to get to her and try again, and if Teague hadn't been there, he would have beaten his chest and dragged her by her hair to the nearest flat surface like a Neanderthal.

Hell, that's what he *had* done! He'd taken her on the floor like an animal. What more proof did he need that he didn't deserve her?

Ever since that night in San Francisco, he'd been trapped in a game of up and down. Take her, save her, take her, save her. It was a miracle her head wasn't spinning off her damn neck with how hot and cold he'd blown.

But she'd told him she loved him anyway.

Why couldn't he just accept that she did, no matter

when she said it to him? What was the problem with her feeling close enough to him when they were having sex to say it then? He felt close enough to her when they were having sex to *merge* with her!

So…couldn't he *try* to accept it?

What if he asked Romy what he should do to be a better person? Already all she had to do was tsk-tsk him to get him rethinking shit like drinking beer in the morning. She could tsk-tsk him some more, couldn't she?

He could stop swearing as a first step. That'd have to go for the baby's sake anyway.

And he could take a few leaves out of Teague's book of saints—ones that didn't involve stealing the guy's interior-design flair. Teague had been to therapy after his sister died, and wasn't ashamed to admit it. So couldn't Matt give therapy a try—deal with his demons that way instead of locking himself in the tower? Wasn't Romy worth at least giving it a go?

What did he *want* out of the rest of his life, anyway? Not to fuck every girl he met the way he'd been doing forever—that was the way to turn into his father. Jesus! Scary.

The rest of his life… Forever… Ha. It was simple, really. His forever was tied up with Romy Allen—that's how all this had started. The baby was his gateway to forever with her. She'd said that night in San Francisco they had a window of opportunity that was like fate. Neither of them had someone in their lives at that precise moment when she needed him, they were together, she needed his sperm, he needed a release.

What if she was right about it being fate?

What if he ignored fate, and *didn't* get her into the

tower with him and she got tired of trying to scale the wall and ended up with Teague?

Teague, who'd met her parents when Matt had not.

Well, fuck that! (Okay, stopping swearing would be a work in progress.) *He* should be the one meeting Romy's parents, not Teague. They were *his* baby's grandparents! And this wasn't petty jealousy, it *wasn't*. It was nothing to do with Teague personally, because he *liked* Teague, he did. No, it was about the past ten years and the past five weeks and…and finding his place in Romy's life and not letting her hate him and…and…and God, he needed a shower and clean jeans and a half-decent shirt and a taxi to Petit Diable.

And Romy, he needed Romy.

CHAPTER NINETEEN

MATT ARRIVED AT Petit Diable forty minutes later and looked in through the glass frontage until he found the Allens.

He watched for a few minutes, assessing the dynamics of the small group and growing anxious without understanding why—unless it was that they seemed so *nice*. Laughing, talking, helping serve each other from the platters on the table, focused completely on each other instead of the potential talent at other tables. Vastly different from the rare get-togethers he endured with his parents, during which the only indication they were a family came from his obvious physical resemblance to them both.

Romy didn't look anything like either of her parents—her father was stick thin and dark, her tiny mother looked like a damn movie star—but you could tell they were a solid unit. Assessing them, he wondered if the way he'd visualized his daughter, as a Matt/Romy combination with hazel eyes and red hair, might be way off the mark.

Something flickered through him like quicksilver—a sense of…disquiet. He stared at Romy's parents, trying to anchor the thought, but before he could latch onto it his view was blocked by servers clearing their table and he realized he'd have a better chance of latching onto whatever was bothering him if he actually joined them.

The moment he entered the restaurant, Romy looked straight at him—as though she sensed him. Her parents swiveled in their chairs to see what she was looking at, Romy dipped her head and said something to them, and next second they were on their feet, beaming at him.

Matt beckoned to the maître d' and after a quick explanation, the guy conducted some weird wordless cross-restaurant communication with Romy, and then he was allowed to make his way to them.

"Sorry I'm late," he announced upon arrival at the table.

Romy's father grabbed his hand and pumped it enthusiastically. "No need for apologies, son," he said.

Matt blocked a start at the "son" a fraction too late, and then started again when Romy's mother opened her arms. Shit. She was going to hug him. He didn't want that. He hadn't earned that. Didn't...*deserve* it.

Matt considered side-stepping her, making an excuse about needing the restroom, but it was too late; he was folded against her. And then that wasn't enough for her: her hands reached up, his head was dragged down and he was kissed soundly on each cheek. Another hug, and he was released, only to have both his hands held, gripped.

"I'm so very glad to meet you, Matthew," she gushed. "I've been wanting to thank you, personally, for what you're doing for Romy." And sure enough, there were tears swimming in her eyes! He wasn't going to cope with this. He shouldn't have come. He didn't belong here. He had to leave. But then she rubbed a rueful thumb against his cheek and said, "Lipstick, my darling, sorry," and his resistance melted because she was adorable.

His place setting was arranged as if by magic, his chair positioned opposite Romy and between her parents, and Mrs. Allen fussed him into his seat.

She smiled at her husband, who was seated on Matt's left. "Pour Matthew some wine, my love." Back to Matt. "Or would you prefer beer? Romy says you like beer."

"Wine," Matt said. "Wine is great, Mrs. Allen."

"Now, Matthew," she chirped on, taking her seat on his right, "none of this *Mrs. Allen* business. My name is Lenore and the handsome gentleman on your other side is Graham. And we should warn you that we're already half in love with you, but if we get too embarrassing give us a stern word and we'll stop." She shot him a little twinkling smile. "Or at least we'll *try* to stop, but I can't promise absolutely."

"Mum!" Romy shook her head. "Matt's not demonstrative."

Lenore reached for Matt's hand. "Matthew can be whatever he wants to be and we'll still love him." She gave his hand a squeeze before releasing it. "We've had our appetizers, I'm afraid, and Romy's already ordered share plates for our main course. But I'm sure we can increase the portions. Romy—shall I call the waiter over and ask for Jules?" Back to Matt. "Jules is one of the chefs here, an old boyfriend of—"

"He knows Jules," Romy put in quickly. "I'll ask Francois to get a message to the kitchen."

Lenore leaned toward Matt conspiratorially. "It's over with Jules, of course. A lovely young man but not for Romy."

Romy got to her feet with a screech of chair. "Mum! Matt doesn't care about my boyfriends."

Lenore raised an eyebrow at her. "I thought you were going to find Francois?"

She waited until Romy had walked over to the maître d', then focused on Matt again. "So! Now! Matthew! Romy may not have told you this, but Graham and I met at university just as you two did…"

By the time Romy returned a few minutes later, Matt had learned that Lenore and Graham had been married for thirty years, that they lived in Barnes (only thirty minutes away from central London but a world away in its "village family feel," which was "perfect for grandchildren"), were planning to renew their vows in two months' time (because "love should be celebrated") and that he was invited to attend the ceremony (because he was "practically family").

So far, so…what? Good? Bad? He had no fucking idea.

Romy took her seat and asked him apprehensively, "Are you okay?" which he assumed meant she had no fucking idea, either.

"Fine," he said, and took a giant sip of wine.

He did his best to keep up with the conversation, but as Romy reached for her water glass, that goddamn platinum ring on her pinky finger flashed, distracting him. Why did that ring bother him so much?

He sifted through his memories of the past ten years of the three of them—him, Romy, Teague—trying to find one that exposed some deep-seated jealousy that would explain his unexpected ring paranoia. The night he and Romy had met three months into their freshman year and they'd almost kissed, but he'd rewound and pushed Teague's barrow instead. Romy asking his advice ahead of her first date with Teague: What should she talk about? The night she broke up with Teague. Her twenty-first birthday dinner—and yeah, Teague producing the ring had seemed an over-the-top gift, but hey, it suited her. The Fourth of July ball at Teague's family estate. Matt had been too busy with one of the other guests— Leah Carnegie-Phillips—to resent Teague monopolizing Romy; Matt had described himself as Leah's bit of rough when he'd told Romy about it, and called Teague Romy's bit of smooth, which had irritated her so much he'd ended up getting her in a headlock and telling her to get over herself—but they'd been friends again within half an hour.

So many memories. Harmless memories.

He heard a clatter and snapped his attention back to the present. Romy had dropped her fork to her plate and was directing a pinch-mouthed headshake at her mother.

What had he missed?

Lenore smiled at him, a faint stain of pink on her cheeks. Remorse. "I apologize. I thought it was all settled."

"It is," Romy said.

"What's settled?" Matt asked, because it was clearly something to do with him.

Lenore looked from Matt to Romy to Matt. "The adoption," she said.

Matt frowned at her, uncomprehending. "Adoption?"

She patted his hand. "There's no difficulty with it, so don't worry that it will be an inconvenience."

"Huh?"

"If you were going to be named on the birth certificate, we'd have to get your consent, and Romy's told us you don't like being bothered with paperwork."

"I don't— Wh—? I thought this baby was—" He looked at Romy. "You're keeping the baby." Not a question—a demand for confirmation.

"Yes, of course I am," she said, flustered. "Mum means when I marry, should my husband want to become…become…"

"The legal father instead of a stepfather," Lenore finished for her. "Romy's birth father *was* on the birth certificate, you see, so he had to give consent, and it took a while to track him down."

"Hang—" Head spinning. He looked to Romy. "You're *adopted*?"

"Yes. I thought…you knew."

"No."

"I guess… You see we don't…don't think of it, we just… I just know Mum and Dad are my parents, even though I do…I do write to my birth mother, so…" She looked ill. Stricken. "It's not a big deal."

Matt stared at her. "Not a big deal?"

"No, that didn't come out right. I mean things…things have changed, so… Oh God."

He was still staring at her, but he couldn't speak, almost couldn't find the will to breathe.

"Matt, this is something we can talk about," she said, and reached across the table for his hand.

He jerked his hand away from her touch, pushed his chair back and stood. "Excuse me," he said. "I have to… have to…go."

Romy made a move, as though she'd go with him, and he shot her a do-not-even-think-about-it look and headed out of the restaurant.

CHAPTER TWENTY

MATT LET HIMSELF into the apartment, went to the bathroom, splashed water on his face and then just stood
there, holding on to the sink. Holding on, on, on.

Was he in shock? It felt like he might be. He needed a
cup of something warm to take the ice out of his veins.
Or someone to hold him and tell him everything would
be okay.

He laughed at that. A harsh, ugly, mirthless sound.
Who was there to do that for him, when Romy was the
architect of his pain?

Funny, he'd been so busy telling himself a baby would
make him irreplaceable to Romy, too busy thinking she'd
always *been* his and always *would* be his, to consider
what he'd actually be to the baby once some other man
came on the scene. He'd just assumed he'd never be *off*
the scene. But now he knew he couldn't act the part of
the benevolent godfather from a world away, smiling
from the sidelines while some other guy lived with his
kid, loved his kid, was loved *by* his kid.

Godfather. What did that even mean? He couldn't remember who his own godfather was—some guy who'd
been a friend of his parents twenty-eight years ago but

hadn't been in their lives for at least twenty years. Easily forgotten.

As *he* would be.

"Aaarrrggghhh!" The cry tore out of him, doubling him over. His child, oh God, oh *God*, his child wouldn't be his. He couldn't breathe; it hurt too much to breathe, hurt so much he wanted to die.

How could Romy think it would be okay for some guy to adopt his kid? How could she tell him she loved him and then give his baby to someone else? How could she sit there with her parents and listen to them tell him *they* wanted to love him, too, and then let them talk about someone else taking his child as though it was as easy as scrawling a signature across a page, cutting him out of the picture?

He raised his head, looked at himself in the mirror. His face was white, bloodless, and yet there was a wildness in his eyes he recognized. His father's wildness, his father's eyes. He wished he could tear the mirror off the wall, smash it and use a piece of the broken glass to cut them out and deny that truth.

But what difference would that make? The evil wasn't in his eyes any more than it was in his red hair. It was bred in him deeper than the bone.

And there it was—the truth of that quicksilver glimmer of disquiet he'd felt when he'd seen Romy with her parents in the restaurant and wondered what his child would look like. The truth was it didn't *matter* if his child was a hazel-eyed redhead or a green-eyed brunette or anything else—what mattered was the hidden stuff, the soullessness he might pass down. The soullessness that wasn't just part of him, but had been actively encouraged by his parents. What right did he have to want to spawn a child let alone raise one, hammered as he was on both sides of the nature/nurture debate?

He heard the door open…close…then nothing.

But he knew Romy. She'd be wanting to talk, ready to convince him that adoption would be a *good* thing, that it was all about *protecting* him, that this way there was nothing that could *impinge* on his *lifestyle*. She'd tell him she'd make sure the child was as happy as *she'd* been with her adoptive parents. She'd say he could still be as involved as he wanted, if he was sure that was what he wanted, as long as there was *certainty* because children *needed* certainty! Well, the best way to give her certainty was to take himself out of the picture altogether. Because Romy, for all her comments about his revolving bedroom door and his jumbo boxes of condoms and the moans, grunts and squeals she was tired of hearing and the women she was tired of him flaunting in front of her, didn't know the half of what he'd seen, what he'd done, what he was.

But it was time she did.

He straightened. Splashed more water on his face. Shook out his hands. Reset his brain.

She was out there, preparing to talk things through. And this time, he *would* talk. He'd tell her everything at last, and end the game of make-believe he'd been playing with her for ten years so that she finally saw him as he truly was: not a superhero, but a soulless, heartless, worthless bastard.

And all it would cost him was his child.

CHAPTER TWENTY-ONE

NERVOUS DIDN'T BEGIN to describe how Romy felt waiting for Matt to come out of the bathroom.

And when he did emerge, nervous ratcheted right up to terrified at the look on his face. She knew, in that moment, she was about to lose him.

So she decided she might as well go straight for the jugular and said, "I love you."

Miraculously, a crack appeared in his facade. It was blink-and-you'd-miss-it—just his hand jerking an inch upward—but it convinced her that Teague was right when he'd said the way to reach Matt was to make him hear those words.

"And before we begin this conversation," she continued, striking while the iron was hot, "I should tell you my parents think you love me, too. Me…and the baby."

"Don't, Romy."

"Why not?"

"Because it's too late."

"It's not even ten o'clock."

"I mean it's twenty-eight years too late."

"I don't…understand."

He sent her a brief, chilling smile, and took his old position on the extreme left end of the couch, waving a hand at her old position on the right. "Then take a seat, Romy, because I'm going to make you."

She did as he bid her, her heart lurching. "That sounds ominous."

"I'm just going to tell you the truth," he said. "It's time you heard it." He took a deep breath, waited a moment and then began. "Earlier tonight, I asked you why I'd never met your parents."

"Y-yes."

"And you said you and I didn't have the kind of friendship that would make such a meeting easy."

"Yes, but I meant—"

"It doesn't matter, Romy. What really matters is why I didn't introduce you to mine."

She said nothing, but she watched him like a hawk.

"You see," he continued, "the last time I took a girl home to meet my parents, I was seventeen."

"Seventeen…" she said, as dread worked its way down her spine. "Gail."

"I should explain that sex was allowed in my parents' house—they were…permissive—so it was assumed that Gail and I would sleep together. It wasn't the first time for either of us, but it was the first time in my bedroom at home and it felt…important. The first night, we professed undying love for each other, the next I gave her a promise ring, like the romantic idiot I was." He laughed suddenly, but it trailed away as he frowned as though trying to recapture a memory. "And then at the end of that week I found her in bed with my father."

Romy, taken aback by the conversational tone of such an obscene utterance, sucked in a shocked breath, then wanted to kick herself when it made him laugh again.

"Yeah, it took me by surprise, too," he said.

"What happened?"

"Oh, it wasn't all that exciting. My father is a charismatic man. He groomed her, seduced her. She was a year older than me, more sophisticated than I was, but she didn't stand a chance. Not her fault—mine, for not warning her what to expect, not protecting her."

"No I mean what happened *after*, Matt. You, Gail, your mother..."

"Well, Romy, my mother was...involved...elsewhere at the time, so she didn't see the point in taking the moral high ground. I, however, made an embarrassing scene. My father didn't see the problem because it was DC, where the age of consent is sixteen, and Gail was two years over it. He wasn't breaking any laws, and it wasn't like he wanted to date her. But he found the whole thing so tedious, he promised to stay away from my girlfriends after that. Gail was dutifully embarrassed—so much so, she cut ties with me and who could blame her? But I learned my lesson and never took another girl home."

She reached out a hand to him.

"I knew you'd do that," he said dismissively. "But I don't need petting. I'm only telling you so you get the full picture of who I am. So...what fun story should I share next?" He shot her a look that got her heart racing. This was going to be bad. "How about the one starring my mother and Teague Hamilton?"

She couldn't find enough air to suck in a breath this time. "No," she whispered. "No, please."

"Don't worry, Romy. Our saint comes out of it with his halo intact. It happened the year of the Fourth of July ball. Wanting to repay the favor, I invited Teague home for Thanksgiving. He was at a loose end because his family was sailing the Mediterranean. Veronica had dragged

Rafael home to her folks' in some desperate attempt to get them to accept him, Artie was getting up close and personal with his first-ever electric drill, and you were off at some Cordon Bleu cooking school. My parents were supposed to be in Florida shooting movies—more on that later—but at the last minute Mom changed her mind. I suspect because she'd seen a photo of Teague and was intrigued by his preppy good looks. Long story short, one minute we were eating turkey, next minute Mom was trying to eat *him*! And I mean *eat* him. Didn't succeed, of course—you know Teague, loyal to a fault. Still, it was… I mean, Teague… Oh God, Teague…" He faltered, shook his head as though trying to get something out of it, took a breath. "Teague pretended it wasn't disgusting, and he…he hugged me." His voice was hoarse, cracked, hitching. "And he t-told me all m-mothers find him irresistible." Another breath. "He h-hugged me! Can you believe that?"

She wanted to reach for him, fold him in, cry for him. But he was already pulling it all together, so she did nothing but sit there, aching for him…waiting for him, as ever.

When he continued, his voice was devoid of life. "So anyway, as you might have guessed, my parents are what you might call highly sexed. If you were a porn aficionado, you'd be aware of their channel, where you'd see all sorts of things that have nothing to do with vanilla sponge cake. Chet and Cherry Carter—real names Kevin and Marsha—why not look them up, expand your repertoire, get a cheap thrill, whatever. It was a popular site when I was a kid, but the appeal has dwindled lately. Dad blames Mom—the MILF thing isn't working so well for her."

"MILF?"

"Mothers I'd Like to Fuck." He made an impatient, chopping movement with his hand. "You understand what I'm saying, Romy?"

"Yes. Your parents like sex—sometimes with people quite a bit younger than they are, and they're porn stars."

"They've been married as long as your parents have, but they've had so many sex partners they'd never remember them all. You can't approve of that."

"I doubt they're seeking my approval."

"How about if I tell you they didn't care what I saw when I was a kid? That nudity was a normal thing in the house so I couldn't bring friends home, that I could watch porn from puberty, that they laughed and told me not to be a prude when I caught them fucking?"

"I know you're trying to get a reaction from me, Matt—why don't you just tell me what it is you want me to say?"

"That you want me out of your life. I want you to tell me you won't let me near your kid."

And all her bravado crumbled. Her eyes welled. "I'm not saying that. I can't say that, because I love you and I want you as the father of my child. No, *our* child. And I wish I could...could tell you what you mean to me. I wish you could understand what a hero you are, to have come through that and still be you."

"I can't *believe* you!" He jumped to his feet, glared down at her. "I'm not a fucking hero. Stop saying it, stop!"

"I'll keep saying it, Matt, because that's what you are. A hero. My hero. Better than Captain America because you're real and you're here and you're trying to save me from yourself. That's what your tower is about—the one with the moat. Not to protect you, but to protect me! To protect *all* of us. But we love you anyway. And I…I know what you mean when you say we're twenty-eight years too late, because I feel like I've been waiting for you for twenty-eight years and it's *too late* to tell me not to wait anymore. I don't want to be saved, you see. I want to be yours."

"You can't be mine! I'm a sex addict, Romy! That's it! That's all there is to me."

"If you were a sex addict, you'd wouldn't have gone without sex for two weeks after my phone call. You'd never have lasted four weeks after I left San Francisco. And you probably wouldn't have lasted Monday to Friday this week, either."

"For all you know I was with another woman last night."

"I know you weren't."

"You can't know that."

"I can, and I do."

He ran his hands into his hair. "Why won't you listen?"

"I will if you say something worth listening to."

"Then hear this, Romy. If you're pregnant, I don't want to see you again. I'll set up the trust fund, and we're done. Will that prove to you I'm not some fucking hero?"

"No, because setting up a trust fund doesn't gel with the whole anti-Christ vibe you're aiming for."

"I'm not joking."

"I never joke about the anti-Christ. So move along. And if I'm not pregnant…?"

"If you're not pregnant, you can consider you've had a lucky escape and find a new donor."

"I don't want a new donor."

"You said you did in that email."

"I lied."

"You...you must see why I have to back out."

"Well, I don't."

"I've just *told* you!"

"You said things about your parents—that's all. And I'm sorry they weren't better role models, but I can't see what that has to do with you impregnating me."

"Bad genes," he said.

"Hmm. I don't think sexual adventurousness is inherited."

"Addiction can be."

"You're not an addict—we already covered that. And in any case, addictions are treatable. Who's to say *I* don't have a wacky sex gene? I mean, there has to be some reason I want to bite some poor unsuspecting man, right?"

"Romy, I'm serious. No more sperm."

She stood, faced him. "Okay then, when we have sex tonight, we'll use a condom. Or I'll use my hands...or my mouth."

He did a double take that would have been funny if she hadn't been so desperate. "I'm not touching you, Romy," he said.

"Now you see, a *real* sex addict would let me take advantage of him."

"I don't want to take advantage of *you*."

"Then do it as a favor. It won't be easy finding a casual sex partner once I'm pregnant, so I'd be grateful if you'd fuck me while I'm still a viable option."

"No."

"Why not?"

"Because you're too vanilla sponge, okay? I've been with women who want it harder than you do, rougher, wilder. What makes you think you can keep me interested even for one night?"

"I don't know if I can keep you interested, Matt. But I'm happy to take the dare."

"I'm not daring you, Romy."

She shook her head at him, as though disgusted. "You talk about vanilla sponge. You rave about your sexual escapades. You throw out words like *addiction*. But it seems to me you're the tame one. If we've barely moved past the missionary position, it's not my fault, it's yours—you've been directing almost all the action. Maybe I *should* choose Teague! Maybe I'll call him tomorrow."

"You do that, Romy," he said, and the blaze in his eyes as he grabbed her hand and yanked her in was electrifying.

He lifted the hand he held, wrenched off her pinky ring and threw it. Romy heard it ping off a wall but she refused to let her eyes follow its trajectory.

"Okay—here's a choice for you," he said. "Go and find the ring…or have sex with me." He released her hand, spun her to face the room, gave her a push. "Where could it be, hmm? I know you want to find it—it's the right choice, so go do it."

She wrenched herself out from under his hands and faced him again. "I know what you're doing, Matt. Trying to make me choose Teague over you because of some stupid idea that Teague's better than you. That's what this is about, isn't it?"

"Yes! Yes! I'm jealous of Teague because he's better than me! Everything about him is better. Better looking, richer, kinder. He's got a family to be proud of. He's a better man, better father material."

"If you really feel that, Matt, then be better for me yourself. Be the man I know you are. The man I love more tonight, knowing what I know, than I loved ten years ago, knowing nothing except that you were made for me."

"I don't *know* how to be better. God, I hope you're not pregnant—I hope it with every breath in my body."

"I saw the cradle, Matt. I know you want the baby."

One of his hands came up, shielding his eyes—but not before she saw the flash of devastation. His breaths were heaving—one, two, three, four. His mouth tightened— long moment—and then the hand dropped from his eyes to reveal blankness again. "That was…boredom. I had to do something while you were at work."

"I *know*, Matt. I know you."

"Go find the ring," he said through gritted teeth. "Choose Teague. You were always meant for someone like him, not me. Never me. You *know* that."

"I'm choosing you."

"If you choose me, it really will be only one night, Romy—that's all, no more."

"So shut up and give it to me," she said, and reached her arms up around his neck, nestling against him.

For a moment, his arms closed around her, tightened… but then he pushed her away. "Not like that," he said. "If you really want to do this, not like that. Not now, I can't stand it."

"Then how?"

"Like this," he said, and grabbed her hard by the upper arms. He shove-shove-shoved her over to the wall until she was backed against it. For one fraught moment he stared down at her, and then he kissed her so hard the corner of her lip split. She thought he'd stop then, and he did. He stepped back, looked at her mouth and then very deliberately leaned down again to lick at the bead of blood. "Now stop me. Tell me you made a mistake choosing me. Tell me you've changed your mind."

"No."

"I'm going to be rough with you."

"Then I'll be rough back."

That seemed to make him furious—so furious, he reached for her dress and ripped it down the middle. He flicked a glance at her body as though what was on display wasn't important, despite the fact she was wearing her best underwear and sheer stay-up stockings. But then, of course he'd seen every kind of underwear on a woman, all degrees of nakedness, stockings in every color and every style.

"Tell me you love me," he demanded.

"Why?"

"So I can remind you that *I don't love you*. It took me ten years to be interested enough to *fuck* you. What does that tell you?"

"That you were scared to lose me."

He flinched, but quickly rallied. "Yeah, well, I did do it in the end because it's what I'm good for and it's all I need. Now get that through your head and leave me the hell alone before I hurt you."

"You won't hurt me."

"I split your lip."

For answer, she grabbed his shirt and tore it the way he'd done to her dress, buttons flying in every direction. "There, are we even? Now will you shut up and do this?"

He grabbed her hands then, wrenched them up, slammed them against the wall, imprisoned them in one large hand.

She surged against his hold—not to break it but to strain her face toward his. "Kiss me, Matt. Hard as you want."

Keeping her hands imprisoned, he put his mouth on hers and savaged it, sucking and licking and biting. She savaged him right back, tugging against his grip.

"I need my hands," she begged. "I need to touch you."

"I want you to do something very specific, Romy. Say yes, and I'll let go."

"Yes…yes…" she panted. "I'll do anything for you… everything…all the things."

He let her wrists go, and instantly her hands went to his fly.

He stopped her. "Not that, this," he said, and grabbed the back of Romy's head, bringing her face to his naked chest. "Bite me, Romy. Through the skin until you draw blood. Your deepest, darkest fantasy."

"Why do you want me to do it?"

He laughed—a taunt in it. "Because you won't, vanilla girl."

"I will!"

"All you have to do is tell me you've changed your mind and I'll let you go. And you go find the ring and we'll be done."

But she shook her head, fierce, and lowered her head to lick across his left nipple. She was not done. She would do this.

His chest muscles tensed. He drew in a sharp breath through his nostrils. "You can't do it, Romy. Admit it."

Her answer was to suck his nipple into her mouth. One of her hands came up, palm resting then rubbing over his right nipple. He started to tremble, and she took courage from that, trailing her tongue up to his pectoral muscle to choose a spot. She measured it with her teeth, and then started licking there. He stiffened—he knew she was preparing him. But a half moment later he relaxed—he'd *forced* that, she knew he'd forced it.

"Do it, Romy," he urged. "Do it. I need it. This pain to cancel out the other."

She stopped, looked up at him. "What other pain?"

"The pain of wanting…" He paused there, closed his eyes. "Wanting what I can't have, what I *won't* have. Do it. I need it."

She was blinking again, but the tears came anyway, unstoppable. She dipped her head to lick again and her tears dripped onto his chest, mixing with the dampness from her tongue. She switched to sucking him, increasing the pressure. Suck, suck, suck, drawing his blood to the surface. And as she did that, she unzipped his jeans, delved a hand into his underwear, gripped him. One, two, three pumps, and he was gasping, then groaning, thrusting himself into her hand. She kept going, urging him with her hand, alternately licking and kissing and sucking his chest to distract him, forcing his words into her mind—*Do it. I need it. This pain to cancel out the other. The pain of wanting what I can't have, what I won't have.*

Oh God, oh God, she had to do it *now*, because he'd be ready to come in just a few thrusts and she wanted to give him a more intense pleasure to replace the pain she was about to inflict. *Do it—get it over with*, and before she could talk herself out of it she closed her eyes and bit down as hard as she could bear to.

Matt stiffened, a strangled "Fuck" erupting from him as she felt the give, the infinitesimal crunch of skin, a metallic tang. Blood—a tiny drop, no more. Enough, it was enough. She dropped to her knees, pulled his jeans and underwear down, took him in her hand again but only to hold him steady for her mouth.

"Don't," he said.

She licked all the way up the shaft, then looked up. "You said you wanted me to suck your cock. And here I am…on my knees for you…ready. I'm not stopping, Matt."

And with that, she slid her mouth over the tip of his cock, rejoicing when his legs went rigid and a cry gargled up from his throat. She started with tiny sucks, just over the tip, as her free hand delved between his legs to cup and press his balls, gently squeezing and releasing. She soon lost herself to the rhythm, to the male smell of him, the velvety feel, playing with speed and pressure until one deeper, harder suck caused him to cry out again, his head flinging back.

He was going to come. She could feel it building. Powerful, glorious. *Do it—let go*, she begged in her mind and next second his hands tightened painfully in her hair and he shouted her name: "Romy! Jesus God, Romy, Romy, arrrgggghh!"

A long, long moment later, when Matt's violent thrusts had stopped and his head was slumped forward against the wall above her, Romy sat back on her heels and looked up at him, licking her lips, tasting him still. Musk, salt, a little hit of lime.

He reached down for her, pulled her to her feet. "Your turn," he said.

CHAPTER TWENTY-TWO

MATT STRIPPED ROMY'S ruined dress from her and dragged her panties down her legs. "Step," he said, when they were around her ankles, "I want your legs wide open tonight." As she stepped, he yanked up his jeans and underwear, fastening them. He didn't intend to stumble over them when he had a point to prove.

He cast a lascivious look at her, lingering on her breasts, which looked ready to burst out of her bra as usual. He nodded at the front clasp. "Undo it," he ordered, and the moment the cups separated he was on her, rubbing and sucking brutally at her nipples. "I want them out...red...raw...aching for me," he said between sucks, and let out a triumphant roar as they came out of hiding one after the other.

He pulled back, looked at them, half-crazed at the sight of them, at the sight of *her*, in her stockings and high heels and nothing else. "Mouths and hands, right, Romy?" he said, and crowded her against the wall before dropping to his knees in front of her the way she'd done for him.

He wrenched at her thighs, opening them wide, and licked hard and long along the length of her. Delicious, fucking delicious. He licked harder, and harder, and when her hands gripped his hair and pulled it the way he'd done to hers, he licked harder still. He wished he could suck the essence right out of her, drink everything inside her, gulp it down.

He tore his mouth away, looked up into her shocked face. "Listen to me," he said, and the urgency in his voice must have communicated his desperation because she nodded once, twice, eager and resolute. "Brace your shoulders against the wall—I'm going to make you come fast."

"Oh God," she said, as her legs trembled in his hands.

He hoisted one of her thighs over his shoulder, giving himself better access. "I want my mouth buried in you so I'm drowning in the taste of your cum," he said. "Understand?"

"Yes."

His response was to lap at her. "Ahhh," he breathed against her sex. "Yes" kiss "good" lick "perfect." He slid his tongue inside her, using it like a small cock. In, out, in out, as her hips twitched in time.

"Keep going," she said, but as though to torment her he pulled out, and when she kicked her heel onto his back in protest he laughed softly and sucked her clit into his mouth while simultaneously tongue-tipping it so hard her protest ended in a gasping scream.

He started to lick seriously then, up and down, side to side, occasionally plunging his tongue into her. He kept her guessing, using tongue and lips, a graze of teeth, but always returning to her clit, growling low in his throat as he suckled it, lusting so badly for its tiny hardness he couldn't be quiet, then using his lips to squeeze around it, then going back to licking over it sure and strong, until she was a moaning mess, jerking against his mouth.

"I'm coming," she gasped. "I'm coming, Matt!" She tensed all over, her gasps becoming breathless huffing sounds, which built and built, her head thrashing from side to side against the wall as she shoved herself onto his mouth. "I'm coooooooomiiing-oooohhh. Oh God, Matt, God, GOOOOOOOOD."

He kept tonguing her, then suckling her, then licking, licking, licking, until her legs went limp, and the thigh on his shoulder loosened. Matt felt her weight give, as though she were about to collapse, and before she could slump to the floor he was up, spinning her to the wall.

"Hands on the wall," he commanded.

With a whimper, she obeyed.

"Now tell me what you want," he said, but he was already insinuating himself between her thighs from behind.

"You, I want you."

"Be specific. Where do you want me?"

"Inside me."

"Be specific, Romy."

"I want your cock in me."

"How?"

"Hard. Rough. Now. Fuck me."

But he didn't plunge straight in. Instead his arms came around her and he rubbed himself against her back. "Let's get you back up there first," he said, plunging his cock between her legs and rubbing it back and forth against her clit.

"Do you like that, Romy?"

"Yes, yes, you know I do."

"Then show me—squeeze me tight."

And so she arched her back, tightening her thighs

around him, thrusting her pelvis back and forth so that
he slid along the length of her.

"What else do you want?"

"I want your hands on my breasts."

His hands came around her, cupped her breasts. "Like
this?"

"Squeeze them."

"Like this?"

"Harder. I want you to do it hard."

As he squeezed, he kicked her legs wider, bent his
knees slightly to give himself extra thrusting power,
then slowly straightened as he guided himself into her.
"Tight and hot and very wet," he said in her ear, and bit
her neck. "Just the way I like it. Now hang the fuck on."

And with that, he pulled all the way out of her, then
slammed straight back in so that she banged forward,
flattened against the wall. Merciless, he yanked her
back. "Take it, take me," he said harshly, and then he
took her hips in his hands hard enough to bruise, an-
choring her. "Ready?"

"Yes, yes, ready, do it."

And he let fly—shoving into her hard, pulling all the
way out, then slamming into her again. "Fuck me back,
Romy, fuck me back."

She leaned forward and backward, hands pushing at
the wall to give her extra leverage while she shoved her
bottom at him, grunting as he smacked into her. But
the pace was too frantic, too forceful, and she ended up
flat against the wall again with Matt against her back,
shoving into her for all he was worth. Soon that wasn't
enough for him, he wanted his fingers on her, too, so
he spun them again and his back was now to the wall.
He jerked her back against him, buried his cock in her

again, thrusting rhythmically as his hands left her hips to go between her legs. One hand held her labia open, the other fingered her wildly, fast, furious, out of control. "I want to make you come so hard you'll never forget it, Romy."

"You, too," she said, and squeezed her internal muscles, as though she'd milk him of everything he had. "I want you to come like that for me. Unforgettable."

And then there was nothing but groans and gasps and grunts and hoarsely whispered words of encouragement, sex words, fuck words, as they sped up, racing, reaching, needing. A keening cry from Romy, a guttural curse from Matt, as the peak rushed and roared at them.

Oh God, God, no sperm, he reminded himself, as Romy's internal muscles convulsed and she started to come. He stayed, stayed, staaaayed until the very last second, and then pulled out of her, jerking once before spilling against her back.

Her head lolled against his shoulder. She was exhausted; he knew it. And so was he. Tired…and unutterably depressed. That damn stinging was behind his nose again. What a way to leave things. Rough sex, his semen on her back, used up.

No. No. He needed something else. He couldn't find the will to deny himself one last thing, something he wanted more than sex, something he needed. Closeness and comfort.

"Romy, darling?" he said, and kissed her temple.

"Hmmm?" Languid, drowsy.

"Come and let me wash you and then…then I want to sleep with you. Just…sleep. With you."

CHAPTER TWENTY-THREE

WHEN ROMY WOKE the next morning, she knew instantly and instinctively that Matt was not only absent from her bed, but that he'd left the flat altogether—and the grief of it almost suffocated her, so that it took a long, long time for her to force her legs over the side of the bed.

When she finally did, the first thing her eyes alighted on was the platinum signet ring on the bedside table. No note, but why would he need to leave a note? The message was obvious: Teague was the man she deserved, and Matt was handing her over to him, as he'd handed her over all those years ago.

She slid the ring back onto her pinky finger, seeing very clearly why Matt was right to say it wasn't jealousy, what he felt about her and Teague. It was more heroic than jealousy. There was something almost ceremonial in his giving her up because he didn't want to defile her.

How hard it must have been for Matt to come to terms with the fact that although he didn't want anyone else to have her, he *did* want someone else to have her. That he not only wanted her, he loved her.

Not that he'd ever tell her that.

That night in San Francisco, he'd said there were better words than *love* for what they had, words that couldn't be *desecrated*. And yes, maybe he'd heard *I love you* so many times it really was meaningless, but she would have given anything to hear those words from him, because they had to be very special for him to be so careful with them.

Well, she couldn't reproach herself with not having thrown herself into the moat and swum like crazy to reach the tower—that was something. But she also knew ten years was long enough to wait for a man who wouldn't let himself have you. A man who pushed and pulled you and tied you up in knots, who made you yearn for impossibilities and then gave them to you only to snatch them away.

But how much easier it would be to let him go if he'd left things at sex against the wall last night. If he hadn't taken her into the shower and washed himself off her like he was a stain. If he hadn't towel-dried her like she was made of delicate glass. If he hadn't gathered her into his arms in bed, and held her close and stroked her hair and kissed her in a way that had nothing to do with sex and everything to do with deep and lonely love.

She took a painful breath…held it…blew it slowly out.

Okay, enough wallowing. Just…enough.

It was Sunday and she had a typical English roast dinner to prepare for Teague if he could be persuaded to join her, because she not only owed him for the steak and ale pie but she needed a friend now more than she'd ever needed one in her life. A friend who could never, ever be more, not because of who he was but because of who he wasn't.

But first, she would clear Matt out of the nursery—a symbolic fresh start.

She strode purposefully to the spare room, but as she

grabbed the pillow off the bed to remove the pillowcase for washing, Matt's scent—the scent under the soap—flooded her, and she stumbled. She couldn't take off the pillowcase. The sheets, either. Because that would mean he was really gone. That what was between them was really over. Not just five weeks of insane passion, but ten years of irreplaceable love.

She looked at the crib, with its misshapen stars and paint drips, and before she knew what she was doing, she'd crawled into Matt's discarded bed, drawn up the covers, buried her face in his pillow, and she was crying like a troll.

CHAPTER TWENTY-FOUR

MATT WAS ON the deck, hungover, drinking beer and not enjoying the view of San Francisco Bay.

It had been two weeks since he'd left London and his need to know if Romy was pregnant was eating him alive.

His heart felt like it had been scrubbed up and down a stone wall until its entire outer layer had been scraped off and it hurt like hell. His head hurt, too, from thinking about her so relentlessly. The only part of him that didn't hurt was his dick, which seemed to have dropped dead. He guessed that was something to be thankful for; his current broken state shouldn't be inflicted upon any woman. But he wished it would give an intermittent pulse so he knew resuscitation wasn't completely out of the question at some future date. Light at the end of the tunnel. Evidence he wasn't going to feel this awful forever.

Okay, he needed more beer.

He wandered into the house he'd decided he hated on the basis that it was too *Teague*-like, and made for the kitchen—which he hated on principle because Romy had never seen it.

He'd just grabbed a bottle from the fridge when the

doorbell rang, and he experienced the first surge of energy he'd had for two weeks. For a moment, he didn't recognize it—and then he was racing for the door, yanking it open, his heart surging…then tumbling.

Not Romy.

The disappointment was bitter.

"What the fuck do *you* want?" he asked his father.

"Is that the best greeting you can manage?"

"For you, yes."

His father laughed. "Aren't you going to let me in?"

Matt didn't move so much as an inch.

"You'll be interested in what I have to tell you," his father wheedled.

Matt turned sharply on his heel—not inviting him in but not barring the entrance—and headed back to the deck.

"I'll take a beer if you're offering," Chet/Kevin said to his back, which was when Matt realized he'd been so eager to answer the door he'd taken his beer with him.

"I'm not offering," he said, without turning around.

Matt took his regular seat, stretching out his legs, leaning back in his chair. Being near his father always made Matt want to occupy more space than usual. "What do you want, Kevin?" he asked.

His father grimaced—he hated being called Kevin but knew better than to ask Matt to call him anything else. "To impart some news."

"So impart it."

"Your mother and I are getting divorced."

Matt waited for surprise to hit, for sorrow, regret, *something*. But he felt nothing.

"She's met someone," his father continued. And then, when Matt still said nothing, "Well?"

"Well, what?"

"Don't you have anything to say?"

"How do you feel about it? About her loving someone else?" Matt finally asked.

His father shrugged. "I doubt it's love that's motivating her. More likely to be because he's ten years younger and hung like a horse. I know—I hired him for a film."

"That's *it*?"

"It's time for greener pastures for both of us."

Matt sat up straighter. "You two have been frolicking in greener pastures your whole fucking lives."

"Thirty years is a long time to stay with the one partner."

Matt thought of Romy's parents, about to renew their vows. "No, it's not," he said. "That's why you *get* married. To stay with someone."

"Yeah, well, I daresay it won't last. I mean, a ten-year age gap? He can do better."

"You're a prick."

"I don't know why you always have to be so hostile."

"Sure you do."

"If you're still bitter about Gail—"

"Don't say her name!"

"—that happened a long time ago. It's not as though you were ever going to marry her."

"A *pathetic* prick."

"Sex is just sex. That shouldn't have come between us."

"Seems like Mom found out sex isn't just sex."

"Matthew, I'll have a replacement for your mother within a week. In my bed, and for the channel. And a fuck really is just a fuck at the end of the day."

A fuck's a fuck.

Matt recalled all the things he'd said to Romy about fucking and he seriously thought he might throw up. He

stared at his father as though he'd never seen him before, the truth coming at him like some sign from the
fucking universe.

Was it really as simple as it suddenly seemed? A matter of asking himself what he wanted his life to be? Because if so, he'd known the answer all along: he wanted
his life to belong to Romy.

He wanted today what he'd wanted from the night
he'd met her: everything, forever. Her thoughts, her
laugh, her touch. He wanted the way she looked and
the way she spoke, the way she smelled. He wanted her
baby to be his. He wanted sex with her, and friendship,
and everything between those things. He wanted every
word either of them could think of for two people who
belonged together, and if they discovered new words,
then he wanted them, too.

And of course he knew the only word for all those
things he wanted. The best word. The only word. The
word was *love*.

"I'm nothing like you," he said wonderingly to his
father. "I'm really, truly nothing like you, and I have no
idea why I always thought I was."

His father let out a bark of laughter. "Funny you
should say that, because we weren't so sure ourselves.
But we had you tested and you're mine all right."

"No, I'm not," Matt said. "I'm not yours and I'm not
hers, either. I would *never* test my child's DNA because
all I want it to be is *ours*. You see, Kevin, I've come to
the conclusion that a family isn't about blood, it's about
love. I don't want to be the bystander in a sexual menag-
erie, I want to be part of a real family. Because I'm *not*
a sex addict even though you tried to make me one, and

I know that sex isn't just sex, that it's a big deal, and it's an even bigger deal when you're in love."

Love—the word burst inside him and he fucking loved it. Loved *her*, with her steadiness and her paperwork and that tiny streak of wild that meant she could try to bite him through the skin but do a piss-poor job of it just because she didn't want to hurt him. He loved her so much he could have died on the spot with the realization of it and died happy.

But his father was laughing dismissively. "Love is a bourgeois emotion."

Matt got to his feet. "Then call me bourgeois, because I feel it and I want it and I'm going to go and get it. So see yourself out, Kevin—I have to pack."

Talk about déjà vu! Throwing clothes in his duffel, grabbing his passport, heading out the door and—

"Shit!" as he whacked straight into someone. He stepped back. "What the *fuck*, Teague."

"Those were going to be my words to you. What the fuck have you done to her?"

"I don't have time to talk. I have to fly to London," he said, and made to barge past.

Teague grabbed his shoulder, stopping him. "Don't you think you've done enough damage?"

"Whatever damage I've done, I'm going to undo it. Now let go."

"You won't undo it in London, because she's not there."

Matt fixed him with a gimlet eye. "Where is she? And don't say at your apartment in Manhattan if you value your life."

"I'm not in Manhattan, dodo."

"You know what I mean. At your apartment, when she should be here."

"As it turns out, she *is* here in San Francisco—albeit not with you."

Matt dropped his duffel bag and stood rooted to the spot, staring at Teague but comprehending nothing.

"Now," Teague said calmly. "Can we go inside and discuss what happens next?"

"*You* go inside and do whatever you like—but first, tell me *exactly* where she is."

"She's here for Lennie. I'm sorry but she doesn't want to see you. That's why she sent me."

"I don't underst—"

"I have a waiver for you to sign."

"Waiver...? Is she... Is she..." He closed his eyes, opened them. "Oh God, she is, isn't she?"

"If you mean pregnant, then yes. And before you try to kill me, no, it's not mine."

"I know that. It's mine."

"Biologically, yes."

"Not just biologically."

"Not just— Okaaay, I see. I think. But my understanding is that you were never going to be registered on the birth certificate so the only way you can gain parental rights is to—"

"Apply to the court for a PR order if she won't work out an agreement with me."

"Been doing some research, I see."

Matt shrugged a shoulder.

"She doesn't want to work out an agreement. And she seems to think you'll be fine with that." Pause. "She wants to move on, Matt."

"Where is she?"

"It won't do you any good to see her."

Matt's hand shot out and grabbed Teague by the throat. "Where. Is. She?"

Teague tried to nod his head.

"Does that mean you're going to tell me?" Matt asked.

Another attempted nod...and Matt released him.

"Jesus, Matt," Teague said, rubbing his neck.

"Sorry."

"No, you're not."

"No, I'm not. So where is she?"

"Ah, geez! This sucks, you know? I'm not supposed to tell you."

"I'll kill you if you don't."

Teague sighed...laughed...sighed again. "If I tell you, it's only because I think you love her."

Matt's jaw tightened. "I do. Now. Where *is* she, goddamn you?"

"She's having lunch with three business associates at a restaurant called Persini's. One of them is probably going to be a client, so don't barge in there being a dick and embarrassing her."

"Shut up, Teague." He turned to unlock the door. "Go in and make yourself a drink." He laughed. "You'll like the place—*that* much I can promise you. But I don't like it and neither does Romy, so if you're looking for a house in San Francisco, make me an offer. Pick a bedroom if you want to stay." Another laugh. "The walls are thick so it won't worry us."

"What does that—? No, don't tell me. But seriously, can't you at least shave before you go and see her?"

Matt thought about it. And then said, "No. It'll take too long."

CHAPTER TWENTY-FIVE

ROMY KNEW THE moment Matt entered the restaurant when her three dining companions' gazes fixed on a point behind her and their jaws dropped.

She estimated Teague had reached Matt's house fifteen minutes ago, so he was here faster than she'd expected. But he was wasting his time.

She refused to turn around, even though the tingling of her skin told her he was barreling toward her, and she stayed stubbornly in place when the smell of his pine-scented soap announced he'd arrived at the table.

"Good afternoon," he said to her companions, his voice sending a quiver through every nerve ending in her body. "Please excuse Romy for a few minutes."

And she found herself lifted out of her chair and—unbelievably—swung up into his arms.

She wanted to tell him to put her down, but one look into his green eyes obliterated every thought in her head so that even the gasps, titters and laughs from throughout the restaurant as he kissed her barely registered.

And then, "God, that felt good," he said, and headed out of the restaurant with her held against his chest and she still said nothing.

"There's an alley at the back of the restaurant out of

the wind," he said once they were outside. "Hang on and we'll go there so I can kiss you properly."

At last she found her voice. "You already kissed me properly."

"So I'll kiss you properly twice. Maybe even ten times. Or a hundred."

"Put me down!" Belated, but hey, she'd said it.

"It's warmer in my arms," he said, and kept walking.

"Matt!"

"Okay, okay, sorry, we're here," he said, and slowly released her so that she slid all the way along his body until she was standing plastered against him—at which point he kissed her again, long and passionately, before pulling back to stare at her face, his mouth quirking up in the same rueful smile he'd worn when he turned up unexpectedly at her flat in London. "I've missed you, Romy!" And yes, that was the same breathless voice he'd used then, too. He was uncertain of her.

Oh God, it was hard to put her hand on his chest and stop him from taking her back into his arms. "You can't do this to me again," she said, and was distressed to hear the wobble in her voice.

"What do you mean? I've never done this before."

"Yes, you have."

"What? I've walked into a restaurant and carried a woman out like a scene in a movie, have I? I'd have sworn I'd remember that. It's better than *The Proposal*, you know, what I just did. Demonstrative. Tell your mother."

"I mean sex."

"I haven't had sex in a restaurant, either—but I'm up for it if you are."

"I mean if you're here to have sex with me again *anywhere*, I can't do it."

"Is it because of the baby? Is it dangerous? What does the doctor say?"

"Because of the—? No! Stop researching pregnancy! It's because of how you make me feel after sex. Like... like I've *taken* something from you. I don't have it in me to go through it again. And anyway, you told me that when a woman says it's over, it's over—no questions asked. So why are you here?"

"Well, that's easy—I'm here because I love you."

Her heart gave one huge thump and then started beating in operatic, percussive surges, making her wonder if she was about to have a coronary. She couldn't speak, could barely think, because Matt—*Matt!*—had just told her he loved her.

"But on the subject of no questions," he went on without seeming to realize the effect his words had had on her, "I find there is, in fact, a question to be asked before I accept it's over. But this is a one-off, won't work with any other woman. It's this: What can I do to make you not want to leave me?"

"Oh, Matt! This isn't fair. I didn't want to leave you— you left me!"

"I know. I'll spend forever making that up to you. I'll even eat Lennie's snails and tell him I like them."

"It's not funny."

"Damn straight it's not. I hate Lennie *and* his fucking snails. Oh, but by the way, we need to work on my swearing. We've got nine months to cure me of the need."

"You're making me laugh, *it's not funny*. I offered you everything I am, in every way I know, and you still left me. I have nothing left to give you."

"Then don't give it to me. Make me earn it. Tell me what I need to do and I'll do it. I'll keep doing it until you tell me to stop. Until you beg me to stop. Until you say, *Jesus, Matt, enough already.* And— Hey! Hey, no crying! No crying or you'll make *me* cry, and I look worse than a troll!"

"You never cry."

"Oh, Romy, I've been crying for two weeks straight."

"You have not."

"In my heart, I have. Tears of blood."

"I thought you didn't have a heart."

"Yeah, well, I was wrong." He took her hands in his. "My heart, as it turns out, was waiting for you." He put her hands, both of them, over his heart. "There it is— you can feel it. It's doing its damnedest to beat itself out of my chest and find a way into yours. Might take some work to get its muscles strong enough to do that, because it's been knocked around over the years. It's not as good as yours, but it wants to be. It's kind of battered but it's trying to heal so that it can beat to the same rhythm as yours every day of our lives." He released her hands, his arms going around her, holding on. "Please, Romy, please!"

"I don't know if I can, Matt," she said, but she was clinging close all the same, her heart yearning to believe. "I need certainty, for me and the baby. I need you to *be* there."

"I've been there for ten years."

"That's different."

"It's not, you know. I've been protecting you for ten years, because I've loved you all that time—but what I was protecting you from was me, and lately I've started to think I'm redeemable. You see, you asked me that night in London to be a better man, but the better man was in there—it was the part of me protecting you. I reckon there might even be a soul in there somewhere if we get a torch and have a good look. Not all black, either." He leaned down for a quick, hard kiss. "What do you say? Will you help me look for it?"

"Okay, let me tally this up. I get the heart. I get the soul. But what about the other thing you said you had to offer?"

"Other thing?"

"The very big thing. I'd want that, too, you know."

He hooted out a laugh. "Oh, hell yeah, you can have the very big cock, that goes without saying—no biting that, though."

She threw her arms around his neck. "Oh, Matt, Matt! I want to kill you and kiss you at the same time."

"Better get the kiss in first, because I know I keep telling you I've done most things, but necrophilia is not on."

"You are *so* not as deviant as you pretend," she said, laughing helplessly.

And then she kissed him, pouring her own heart and soul in there, and maybe she was crazy, but she was sure she could feel them connecting with his.

When she pulled back, he cupped her face in his hands. "You know, Romy, if I could go back in time, I'd kiss you that first night, the night we met, and I'd never stop. I'd tell you I love you and never stop. Never, ever stop." Another kiss. "Just one thing I want to clarify: Isn't it customary for the girl to say *I love you* back to the guy who says it to her? Because that would be you saying it to me, in case you're in any doubt."

"I thought you didn't want to hear it."

"Ah, hell! Of course I want to hear it."

"What happened to sex being just sex?"

"I'm too bourgeois for that!" he said, and kissed her

yet again. "I want to be able to do that, to press my mouth to yours and know it might end up with me buried inside you…or it might just as easily not. It's better than sex…and worse than sex, because you can hurt me in so many ways, none of which have anything to do with sinking your teeth into my skin in a moment of kink. But on the subject of kink, and specifically necrophilia, I should just give you a little warning that I might actually keel over and die in a minute if you don't tell me you love me, and you said something once about the need for sex as a pregnant woman and you won't want to do it with a dead guy, will you?"

"Fine—I love you!" she said, laughing, laughing, laughing.

"Okay, now I'm going to have to kiss you again," he said, and drew her into his arms. "But you know that thing I said about being able to kiss you and not have it go any further? I meant that, I really did, but I have one confession to make on behalf of my very big cock. It's gone rogue on me. It's refusing to let anyone touch it except you—it won't even let me take it in hand myself. So you're going to have to take it in hand for me—well, hand, or mouth, or body, I'm equal opportunity when it comes to my cock. And when I kiss you, it's going to start clamoring for attention. So just be aware, okay?"

"You're depraved."

"And aren't you the lucky one?"

"Yes," she said, and snuggled closer, "I guess I am."

"Okay, one rogue penis coming up," he said, and he lowered his mouth to hers.

* * * * *

COMING SOON!

We really hope you enjoyed reading this book. If you're looking for more romance, be sure to head to the shops when new books are available on

Thursday
23rd August

LET'S TALK
Romance

For exclusive extracts, competitions
and special offers, find us online:

- ▪ facebook.com/millsandboon
- ▢ @millsandboonuk
- ▸ @millsandboon

Or get in touch on 0844 844 1351*

For all the latest titles coming soon, visit
millsandboon.co.uk/nextmonth